Farewell, Mahatma

Farewell, Mahatma

Stories

Devibharathi

Translated from the Tamil
by N. Kalyan Raman

HARPERPERENNIAL

An Imprint of HarperCollins *Publishers*

HARPERPERENNIAL

First published in English in India by Harper Perennial 2014
An imprint of HarperCollins *Publishers*
4th Floor, Tower A, Building No. 10, DLF Cyber City,
DLF Phase II, Gurugram, Haryana – 122002
www.harpercollins.co.in

This edition published in India by Harper Perennial 2024

2 4 6 8 10 9 7 5 3 1

P-ISBN: 978-93-5699-949-7
E-ISBN: 978-93-5029-880-0

Typeset in 11/14 Adobe Garamond Pro
by Jojy Philip, New Delhi

Printed and bound at
Thomson Press (India) Ltd

FSC
www.fsc.org
MIX
Paper from
responsible sources
FSC® C010615

This book is produced from independently certified FSC® paper
to ensure responsible forest management.

To
my beloved sister and French author,
Pascale Kramer

Contents

Farewell, Mahatma

From the gentle screech of its hinges, Gandhi knew that someone was pushing open the door to his room. Then he heard the shuffling of feet moving closer with each careful step. The Mahatma closed his eyes and pretended to be asleep.

It had to be Dhaniklal – an old man who was by far the most vigilant among the inhabitants of Birla House; Gandhi's principal secretary, someone who took more pride in calling himself disciple than secretary; who believed that ministering to the great man was equal to serving the nation. Dhaniklal's sole duty consisted of watching over the Mahatma through the night, without catching a wink of sleep, from a very small room situated directly opposite his chamber. He entered Gandhi's room at least thrice every night and made sure all was well with him. Even a gentle whimper from Gandhi made Dhaniklal very nervous. Gandhi had once asked him playfully, 'Why this sleepless vigil over me, Dhaniklalji? Do you wish to be a witness when I die?'

Dhaniklal was alarmed. 'You will never die, Bapuji,' he had said. 'The future of this nation has been entrusted in your merciful hands.'

Gandhi sighed. 'I won't die so quickly, Dhaniklalji,' he had replied. 'My duties aren't fulfilled yet. My struggles, too, are very long ones. I am condemned to live for as long as I am needed. If, by chance, God decides to take me back sooner, no one can anticipate that moment, not even you. Coughs and moans will never portend my death, Dhaniklalji. My death will be noiseless. At the dawn of a springtime morning, a small bird nesting at the top of a very tall red cedar tree in the centre of Delhi will wake up and announce my death to the world. Dhaniklalji, everyone – including you – will be fast asleep then. So stop worrying and get some sleep.'

But Dhaniklal was never able to sleep properly. Gandhi, when he woke up at dawn, would see Dhaniklal asleep with his head resting on the edge of his bed. So as not to disturb him, he would get up without making a sound and go to the bathroom. Dhaniklal would be fast asleep till Gandhi had finished writing his letters. Urged by instinct perhaps, he would wake up just before Gandhi set out on his morning walk. Later, during prayers and whenever Gandhi was engaged in discussions inside his room, Dhaniklal's eyes would glaze over with sleep. Whenever Gandhi saw Dhaniklal in this condition, his heart would overflow with kindness and compassion.

But Gandhi also suspected that he was gradually losing the ability to handle his annoyance caused by Dhaniklal's vigils. He was constantly worried that he might inadvertently say hurtful things to Dhaniklal. He regretted having to pretend to be asleep whenever Dhaniklal entered his room, merely to evade the latter's questions. His eyes communicated distaste whenever he saw Dhaniklal. He examined his aversion closely. He disliked not only Dhaniklal, but also Nehru, Patel, and everyone who indulged in rioting; in truth, it was also a symptom of Gandhi's self-hatred.

That night, as the door hinges screeched and Dhaniklal's footsteps came closer, he awoke. 'Dhaniklalji, you haven't gone to sleep yet? Why are you up and about at midnight? I have begged you so many times not to trouble yourself over me. You people are making me feel guilty. Our duty right now is to do something for our grief-stricken people. That would be far more worthwhile than ministering to me, Dhaniklalji!'

'Please forgive me, Bapuji! I came here because it was very cold in my room. You could use this khaddar blanket to cover yourself, surely?' Dhaniklal covered Gandhi with the thick blanket he had brought with him.

Gandhi flung the blanket aside and sat up. 'I can't get any sleep. You are keeping me awake for nothing. And I haven't done anything useful the whole day – just meetings, discussions and interviews. I could have gone with the volunteers to collect blankets for those poor people in the camps. I am living here like an emperor while children, women and old people are in great agony.'

'Our volunteers are doing their job properly, Bapuji. There is no reason to fret. Hundreds of sheets and blankets were distributed to the refugees today.'

'Thank you for bringing me a piece of good news. Were they distributed fairly to everyone?'

'Yes, Bapuji, they were distributed evenly to all camps.'

Gandhi smiled. 'People are eager to help, aren't they? It's so gratifying to hear that. I have always said that God is full of mercy.' In his heart, which was much aggrieved by the endless riots, hope began to sprout and grow. The Mahatma believed that his recent fast had not been in vain. He stood up, liberated suddenly from weariness, sleeplessness and fatigue. 'Dhaniklalji, will you drink some hot water? Why don't we chat for a while?' He walked towards the kitchen. Dhaniklal followed him anxiously and offered to help. 'All right. Tell me everything that happened. I am keen to hear it all.'

Dhaniklal was full of zest. He tried to elaborate on those incidents out of the day's happenings which he thought might please Gandhi. He began with how happy the residents of the camps at Turkman Gate and Chandni Chowk were to see the volunteers.

During his visit there a couple of weeks ago, the Mahatma had seen firsthand the pathetic conditions in which the refugees lived. A large number of little girls had sought refuge in the camp at Turkman Gate. He could never forget the twelve-year-old Muslim girl he met there. She told him how her parents had been attacked and killed right in front of her. Rioters had surrounded their settlements around midnight. In order to save the residents of these settlements, her father, a satyagrahi, had fallen at their feet and begged them to have mercy on his people. She could never forget her father's face as he stood before those armed goons, palms folded together in a pleading gesture, said the girl. They chopped off his praying hands, first one, and then the other.

Her mother tried to save her. Hurriedly, she streaked the girl's forehead with vermillion and urged her to chant, 'Jai Sri Ram!' If you do that, the rioters will spare you, and then you can flee elsewhere and survive, her mother had told her; but she refused to do so. 'Allah-hu Akbar' was what she said to them instead.

'Did they let you go?'

'They wanted my body. They dragged me along. For nine days, they kept me confined in their vehicle and raped me. After that, taking me for dead, they flung my body by the side of the road and went away. Then I made my way alone to this camp. I had no identity left at the time. I met many little girls like me. We all looked the same, with our minds in the same state, all of us bleeding. I had even forgotten my name.'

When Gandhi asked him, 'Did you meet that child, Dhaniklalji?' the man fumbled. When he saw Dhaniklal struggling to retrieve facts from memory, Gandhi was worried he might end up lying. 'All right, go and lie down. I am very tired,' he told his helper. Gandhi himself lay down on his bed. As Dhaniklal was preparing to leave, Gandhi saw a look of amusement on his face.

'What did you recall, Dhaniklalji?'

'Forgive me, Bapuji. I could not control my laughter. Oh god! What a great man this Bhagwaticharan turned out to be! I was simply amazed. He was an exact copy of the original, wasn't he? Can such things happen? So clever, this Bhagwaticharan is!' exclaimed Dhaniklal with a belly laugh.

Gandhi observed him in silence. Then the expression on Dhaniklal's face dimmed and settled. Resting his head between his knees, he began to recount everything. 'You know him, don't you? That young Bengali is your disciple. He's come to Delhi only to meet you. Many have spoken glowingly about the work he has done in Calcutta. He is young, most probably in his late thirties. I think he shaves his head every day. But that moustache and those eyebrows…' As he spoke, laughter welled up again in Dhaniklal's throat.

'Listen, Bapuji. We were feeling extremely dejected. No one came forward to help us, not even affluent Gujaratis. The songs we played at the gates of mansions failed to move anyone's heart. By afternoon, we had only collected a few rags. We felt miserable. We begged them to be charitable towards those poor, riot-affected people who continue to suffer in the camps. No one took pity on them, Bapuji. Only an old man, who appeared to be a destitute himself, gave us his vest. He came forward without being asked and gave it to us. That was a grand moment. It was a moment when we recovered the hope we had given up by then.'

'Yes, it was indeed a grand moment! That rag was a sign of

our success, wasn't it, Dhaniklalji?' The Mahatma intervened elatedly. Dhaniklal didn't mind the interruption. The excitement of approaching a thrilling stage in his story showed on his face.

'Then all of us saw how he crossed himself. Paying no attention to our expressions of gratitude, he mumbled a Psalm about Jesus as he moved away. We continued our journey. The winter sun was burning our faces. And our journey was even harder than before. Nobody paid us any attention. What happened then was unbelievable. Bapuji, listen to this! We were passing through a middle-class locality. A few people followed us, just to watch the spectacle. We walked on, singing "*Raghupati Raghava Raja Ram*". Then we heard a loud roar from behind us – *Mahatma Gandhi ki Jai! Victory to Mahatma Gandhi!* – and looked back in surprise. God, I still can't believe the sight that greeted us. Like Christ, he was walking towards us! The Mahatma! None of us believed otherwise. He looked exactly like you, a genuine copy. "Bapuji," we greeted him, still amazed. While he smiled at us gracefully, he also paid his respects to the people who were crowding around him. People drew close to him with a kind of yearning. I saw how unbearably happy they felt at touching his pure white khaddar robe and his bony hands. Then one by one they started to touch his feet. People came running out of their houses and through narrow alleys, and crowded around him.'

Gandhi was listening to Dhaniklal in amazement and confusion; he tried to intervene. But Dhaniklal was describing the events with irrepressible enthusiasm; Gandhi simply couldn't draw the man's attention towards himself.

'Then he began to address the crowd. His voice – just like yours, very gentle but firm – urged everyone to help those who had taken shelter after being subjected to atrocities and hunted down. He repeated the same sentences that you had spoken earlier, about the morality of living, in a voice very much like yours! The duties that we must fulfil, the discretion we must show during turmoil, the patience we must observe during times of crisis, the sense of guilt that must be active inside each one of us – he repeated verbatim all your noble precepts, in the same tone of voice, a perfect imitation! I imagined that his talk was the divine counsel of Bhagavad Gita or Jesus Christ's Sermon on the Mount. People were listening incredulously to everything he said. As if under a spell, they brought out the best blankets and sheets they owned and started to pile them up at his feet. With an unchanging smile, he blessed them all.'

Dhaniklal had grown very tired. Still, the urge to finish recounting everything kept him going.

'Shortly after that, my patience ran out. With difficulty, I made my way through the jostling crowd and drew near him. You won't believe this, Bapuji! I recognized him immediately. Standing very close to him, I whispered, "Aren't you Bhagwaticharan?" He smiled serenely without replying. Bapuji, that smile was exactly like yours!'

The mansion was steeped in silence. The hour was past midnight. The night was bitterly cold.

Gandhi was very tired. He wanted to lie down and sleep for a few hours at least. He wondered if he should continue walking. He had innumerable things to think about. The inconclusive debates held throughout the day had exhausted him. It seemed to him that everything was getting out of hand, and very fast. A tiny sliver of hope had survived, though. There had to be some kind of resolution to every problem, after all! Earlier in the afternoon, when he had been arguing with Patel, he hadn't been able to control his emotions. 'What on earth are you thinking, Sardar?' Gandhi had stood up from his seat. He recalled with distaste how his body had trembled and his face had perspired profusely.

Alarmed, the Iron Man had tried to explain himself and seek Gandhi's forgiveness. 'Bapu, I believe we could even discuss these things again. Truly, we don't have anything to hide from you.' His voice was tinged with sadness. Rising to his feet, he glanced at his wrist watch over and over again, as though looking at it for the first time. Then he resumed his argument. Patel's secretary went on retrieving evidence from the files he had brought along and was handing them to Patel. In his hurry, he even tore off a couple of pages. This act brought profound sorrow to Gandhi's heart; it led him to imagine the act of tearing a child's limb from its body. He told Patel how he felt and requested him to stop. 'There is a way of handling these sheets gently, don't you think?'

On hearing this, Patel burst out laughing. He took the files from his secretary and held them gently. But when he started explaining, he was not able to control his fervour. The Iron Man began to tear out pages in even greater haste than his secretary. 'It's getting late!' he muttered, as if to himself, as he unfurled and held those sheets before his face. Running his thick index finger over important lines, he read out, in a loud voice, important phrases from the page to lend strength to his arguments.

Whenever he spoke to Gandhi, Patel constantly tried to observe the rules of tact and humility; even so, he inadvertently raised his voice now and then. He had no option but to ask for Gandhi's pardon each time.

Before long, a few more secretaries and assistants had arrived. The Mahatma observed that each man had brought an enormous load of files with him. Displaying an incredible degree of discipline and decorum, they did not speak to one another; nor did they even glance at one another. Gandhi noticed that there prevailed, nonetheless, the most precise coordination between them. The anxieties and diffidence normally displayed by civil servants of a newly independent country were not at all evident among them. Most of them resembled Patel in their age and bearing. Except for Patel, all the others wore a jacket and tie in the English style. When Gandhi asked him, 'Didn't you tell these government servants that they should wear only khaddar?' Patel blushed in embarrassment, like a woman.

Then he resumed his explanation. Finally he said, 'You should find a resolution to these matters, Bapu. Give us a solution that can be implemented practically. We are only too willing to take immediate action.' Patel was more or less pleading with Gandhi. 'There is no other alternative for us, Bapu! These actions are unavoidable. If you like, I can hand over my responsibilities to someone else; but these would remain unavoidable for that person too.'

'Unavoidable… no other alternative… fine phrases, these are!' muttered Gandhi to himself, alone in the darkness of his room. When Dhaniklal had taken leave of him the previous night, he had also used the same phrases. Gandhi recalled those phrases and the way he had narrated that 'funny' story. Dhaniklal's voice and facial expressions, along with his chortling at the end of the story, his belly shaking with laughter, rose before his mind's eye. The face of 'Mahatma' Bhagwaticharan also surfaced in his imagination.

A young Bengali man who looked exactly like him. Dhaniklal had described him in such minute detail! From Dhaniklal's description, Gandhi, who had never set eyes on that man, could imagine him quite vividly. Apart from his gentle voice, kind smile and serene gaze, Gandhi was even able to picture the wrinkles on the youth's belly.

Look: people are milling around Bhagwaticharan, greeting him and shouting slogans. *'Mahatma Gandhi ki jai! Mahatma Gandhi ki jai!'* Mahatma Bhagwaticharan gives them his blessings. The crowd is ecstatic: it roars, screams and, overwhelmed by emotion, dissolves into tears. The Mahatma talks to them, makes an appeal, gives instructions. Several people rush towards him and touch him. One man grabs his shawl and runs away. The Mahatma calls him back and gives him his dhoti as well. Now he stands stark naked before all. 'Lord, why have you forced me to roam naked inside this lovely garden?' He is ashamed. He runs, trying to escape from them. He is chased by one and all. One man plucks hair from his moustache and stashes them away. Another pulls out his fingernails and flees. Yet another man attempts to extract his teeth.

The Mahatma can't bear the pain. 'Oh god,' he screams, and shouts for help. A policeman who has been watching everything from a distance ambles over to him slowly. 'Why are you shouting like this?' he asks roughly, giving the Mahatma a hard slap on his left cheek. The Mahatma shows the policeman his right cheek. The policeman slaps him on his right cheek too. The Mahatma keeps showing him both his cheeks by turns, one after the other. The policeman slaps the Mahatma tirelessly. There is a spurt of blood. The few stray teeth that were left in his mouth have come loose. His eyeballs have popped out of their sockets. The crowd scrambles to grab them. The Mahatma's vision grows dim. Suddenly, it is pitch-dark everywhere. 'I am not Mahatma Gandhi – I am Charan, a Bengali named Bhagwaticharan!'

Gandhi involuntarily touched his eyes. He was breathless. He lay down exhausted on the bed and closed his eyes.

When he opened his eyes again a little later, the room was bright with light. Gandhi saw irregular shafts of light crisscrossing his room. Has morning dawned already? Have I overslept, breaking my lifelong habit of rising early? Then it must be a sign of death coming closer. Now it's time to accept my old age. I am 78, after all! The Mahatma smiled to himself.

Where is Dhaniklal? I can't see Manu either! That little girl invariably wakes up before me.

After rolling up his bedding, Gandhi was about to begin his morning ablutions when he heard some agitated voices. Wondering who or what it could be, he opened a window and looked out. He froze in shock and horror. Outside the tall mansion, not very far from it, the city of Delhi was ablaze.

People were running pell-mell in all directions. Gandhi saw them being hunted down with murderous fury by a mob of ten to fifteen people, armed with deadly weapons. Unable to bear his own agony, he shut his eyes tight. Losing all hope, he slumped down on the wooden chair in his room.

Where did it all go wrong?

Who is responsible for this… Hindus or Muslims? Who is whose enemy? Who is going to be slaughtered by whom? Who is going to survive? To settle which score has this frenzy been unleashed? Is it the history of the past millennium which is guilty? But then, we have travelled so far ahead of it! Who is responsible for this violence which is being stoked just when the world is felicitating us as a people who have won their freedom solely by the strength of their spirit, without taking up arms? Am I the guilty party? As a philosopher, have I repudiated the truth? Would a resolution have been reached if I had allowed people to go their own way? Could the killing and bloodshed have brought us peace? In a way, it is indeed a possibility. When the other side is completely wiped out, what can possibly hamper peace? After that, wouldn't this innate blood-lust be directed, out of necessity, at one's own brethren? Is violence man's inborn trait? Is non-violent struggle contrary to the laws of nature?

The principle we relied on when we launched this enormous struggle – is that very same principle in error now?

'Dhaniklalji, where have you gone? And Manu? Wake her up too. No one seems to be around at this harrowing time!' Hollering, Gandhi tried to get up and open the door. He could not. Someone had latched it from the outside.

'Where are you, Dhaniklalji? Who has done this?'

He opened the window on the right, and through it, glanced at the main gate of the mansion; his blood froze. Countless people had gathered on the other side of the mansion's massive iron gate – hundreds of poor people in a half-dead state, recent victims of a murderous attack.

'Bapuji… Bapuji…!'

'Save us, Bapuji…!'

'Oh god…!'

'When Bapuji is here, why should we feel dejected? Guards, please call Bapuji.'

'Fool, open the door. Later, Bapu won't ever forgive you.'

Gandhi rushed towards the door again.

'Dhaniklal…! Anybody around? Why did you lock this door? Please open it. Invite them all inside! Don't burden me with the guilt of this unpardonable crime…! Dhaniklal, come here!'

Again he rushed to the open window.

Carrying torches and lethal weapons in their hands, the rioters who had come in pursuit slaughtered the unarmed innocents ruthlessly. And amid the river of blood and bodies strewn helter-skelter on the ground, little girls were being raped. Gandhi could do no more than silently witness these atrocities, clutching the window bars and resting his face on them like a lifeless corpse.

'Bapuji, Bapuji, why have you abandoned us, Bapuji?'

It was only towards the end that the miracle occurred. From inside the mansion, racked by a profound sorrow, 'Mahatma' Bhagwaticharan arrived. Now the mansion's tall gates were opened wide for him to pass. Accompanied by guards, the Mahatma walked very slowly and reached the bodies lying on the ground. Two or three half-dead people tried to rise on seeing him, and he attempted to console them with words full of kindness – Mohandas Karamchand Gandhi's eyes witnessed it all.

Consciousness was slipping away from him.

Gandhi realized that death's final chapter, made up now of very few pages, lay open in front of him. By the time he finished reading it, death would have come looking for him. Would it come after him, really? Was it not something he should himself seek and attain? When a man's dreams for living are at an end, he begins to seek death. What he could not communicate through his life, he wishes to convey through death. So he chooses to die, thought Gandhi.

All this time, he has considered living an important duty. He has to live out his entire lifespan – that is, 125 years.

For him, longevity has never been a mere fantasy. He has fashioned the habits and practices of his life in accordance with that necessity. As in his soul, the Mahatma has infinite confidence in his body too. He has never been afraid of dying. Only a few days ago, when they heard a bomb exploding near the prayer hall, Manu flew into a panic. To that extremely frightened child, he offered consolation, telling her in order to calm her down that the bomb might have exploded during training exercises at a nearby military camp. He has no doubt that the explosion was targetted at him. The killers are lurking very close to him.

Death is tracking and following him through his 'footprints'. He is quite willing to hand himself over to it. The secret messages that death has been sending his way he receives with a smile. He mocks death, dares it too. At his age, even the fasts that he undertakes are his battle cries against death. Whenever he fasts, everyone goes into a panic, wondering if he might die this time. Doctors examine him. They accept his conditions in exchange for getting him to sip a little fruit juice, conduct peace marches, shake hands with one another, embrace ardently, and pray to god. Later, everyone puts their signatures on the agreement papers and hands them over to him; then they fetch him a glass of fruit juice and urge him to drink. He drinks it with a sense of satisfaction and reaches a compromise with death. Then the Mahatma is lost in his dreams – dreams of his empire, of lasting up to 125 years.

The old routine plays out with scarcely a change. He gets up as usual at three o'clock in the morning, completes his morning ablutions, writes letters, composes essays for *Harijan* and other journals, goes for his morning walk, eats a meal of groundnuts and goat's milk, meets everyone who has sought him out, confers his blessings on everyone. As usual, the ministers meet with him, seek his advice and guidance, and blow their own trumpets. Prime Minister Nehru calls on him, along with Sardar Patel. The Mahatma is delighted to see the two leaders standing together, shoulder to shoulder. Everyone participates in the prayer meetings held every evening. Verses from the Koran, Holy Bible and the Bhagavad Gita are read out and listened to; then they are sung by the crowd in one voice.

Raghupati Raghav Rajaram,
Patitpavana Sitaram
Ishwar Allah tero naam,
Sab ko sanmati de Bhagavan

The many charades of death, its different disguises.

Then, more news of rioting arrives from somewhere through someone or the other. He watches as the black smoke rising from human bodies set aflame spreads over and clings to the windows of his room. He listens to bomb explosions and cries of distress. Only then does he go silent like the monkey figurines he keeps in his room. He closes his eyes, shuts his ears too. But more and more reports keep coming in, drilling into his ears. Reports about how satyagrahis who have risen to power are indulging in corruption and scams; how quarrels between Nehru and Patel are escalating every day – he hears them even when his ears are still shut. 'It's either me or him…' Proclamations, threats, complaints, warnings, challenges…!

Satyagrahis are now demanding the wages of sacrifices they have made.

Above all, he is most worried about the future of Delhi and the independent republic. The monkey figurines in his room seem to mock him. So death, which has grown tired after trying on various disguises, stands before him now in the shape of a genuine copy of himself.

'Victory to Mahatma Bhagwaticharan! Victory to Mahatma Bhagwaticharan!'

'This is a cheap trick,' the Mahatma spoke out aloud.

It is cheap, and cowardly as well. It is also a challenge to his self-respect. Death is trying to transform his life into its own message! It is in facing this challenge that the intrinsic meaning of life is hidden. Death too is like life. There could be no greater insult to life than relinquishing the right to choose death. Such are his reflections.

All his life, the Mahatma has immersed himself in myriad fantasies about death. It must be an event full of poetic feeling and courage. His long-cherished dream is for one of his extended fasts to bring his life to an end. There can't be a better opportunity for a satyagrahi, he thinks. He knows he could be killed, too. He did not really pay heed to the sounds of bomb explosions heard near the prayer hall. Death from such an explosion would be honourable. He is quite ready and willing to stand before them stark naked. Of all the defining traits a satyagrahi must possess, courage to choose death is the most important. Sages encounter death with a smile. Death is defeated by them. Then they come back to life and receive the boon of immortality.

Like Jesus Christ; like his teacher, Tolstoy. Their lives are his sole inspiration, their lives and their deaths.

Both had accepted death willingly and heartily. They had engendered their murderers from their own lives. The journey that Tolstoy undertook from Yasnaya Polyana to Astapovo was no less than the journey that Jesus had undertaken to Mount Calvary, carrying death on his shoulders. Gandhi recalls the first time he had read about Tolstoy's journey. He was able to read through those pages only with sighs and a deep sadness.

Later, the same pages seemed very different to him. He had read them over and over again. He had thought that Tolstoy could not have chosen a better way to die. It was a more poetic death than all the other deaths in this world. Gandhi could never forget that snow-clad morning when Tolstoy set out from his mansion.

Each time he woke at dawn, the memory of Tolstoy would come to him. It was most probably at that hour that Tolstoy left that famous mansion in Yasnaya Polyana. After he was brought to Birla House, the lines came to life again in Gandhi's mind, more vivid than ever before. Birla House was indeed no different from that mansion in Yasnaya Polyana. Like Tolstoy, he was also housed in this mansion in the condition of a prisoner. Like Tolstoy, he too longed to get away from there.

Yes, he must get away. He must go back to the scavengers' colony where he once lived – or to his ashram. But all his disciples were sure to follow him there. They would then confine him, either as a prisoner or as god, and post a couple of armed guards to stand stiffly at the entrance. Then it would be the same old story: letters, meetings, blessings and counsel; and in the evenings, prayer meetings. It was truly a fine arrangement!

A god who has been taken prisoner! If he wants to get out, he must follow closely in Tolstoy's footsteps. He must discover his own railway station, his Astapovo outside this city famed for its ancient glories.

No doubt about it: history makes an exact copy of itself, sentence by sentence, leaving out not even a single letter.

At five o'clock on the morning of 29 October 1910, Tolstoy, then eighty-three years of age, left the mansion he had been living in since he was born. A snowstorm was blowing. After abandoning his relatives, he wandered all across the railway tracks of Tula Gubernia, accompanied by his servant of many years, Makovitsky. He was discovered on November 3 inside a shabby and decrepit second class compartment of a train, which was on its way from Volavo to Rostov-on-Don, and was taken off it at a very small station en route called Astapovo.

With the help of the station master and Tolstoy's youngest daughter, Alexandra Lvovna Tolstoy, who had come in search of her father, Makovitsky arranged for Tolstoy, who was suffering from a severe bout of pneumonia, to get off the train. They put him up in the station master's room for the next three days. Almost immediately, the attention of the entire world came to be focused on that small, obscure railway station. Newsmen who had arrived there from all over Europe to provide advance bulletins on the death of one of the world's greatest men waited for three whole days. Back in their offices, their editors had prepared his obituaries, which were ready to be printed. Telegraph stations were working round the clock. 'Leave me alone. I am going to a place where no one will bother about me.' With these words, spoken at five past six on the morning of November 7, the great man breathed his last.

When Gandhi walked out of Birla House, it was a quarter to four in the morning. Unlike his teacher, he set out all alone. He had decided to take Dhaniklal with him but later, he changed his mind. Gandhi had not been able to spot him after eleven in the night. When there was no response to his repeated calls, he went to Dhaniklal's room, looking for him. Even Manu was not there. Susheela had taken the young girl with her the previous night.

When she returns in the morning, the child might be upset at not finding me here, thought Gandhi.

The others were fast asleep. The mansion was engulfed in silence. Gandhi took only a copy of the Gita with him. He did not see any guards at the entrance. Since the gates were open, he was able to slip out quite easily. Worried that he would be recognized if he walked down the broad avenue dressed only in his usual waist cloth and carrying his trademark walking stick, he hurried on. The deserted streets were of great help to him. Dewdrops fell incessantly from the trees. A wall of mist had shrouded the light that trickled from the occasional lamp post. The cold drilled into his bones. He thought he should have brought a blanket.

The snowfall in Yasnaya Polyana would have been thicker.

He had made no plans at the time of his departure. He thought he would reach a nearby railway station and then start his journey from there. He had only an hour's reprieve at the most. Soon they would discover that the 'the parrot had flown the coop'. Tolstoy had left a letter for Sophia Andryevna; he too could have left a letter behind, explaining the reasons for his departure.

Was it hatred that stopped him from writing such a letter?

Not hatred, but love must be the reason underlying my departure. Only if it is love would my going away be meaningful. If this departure is the result of hatred, then I am not a satyagrahi, I can only call myself an incomplete soul, thought Gandhi.

On the pavements flanking both sides of the road, Gandhi saw countless humans, their clothes barely enough to cover them, lying huddled in the biting cold. He wondered if his departure would bring about any change in the condition of these people. He felt confused. Was Bhagwaticharan right in doing what he did? If the sheets and blankets he had collected could have mitigated the suffering of at least a few among these people, how could anyone be critical of his work? But he has lied, impersonated me and cheated the public. Is it possible to reassess such misdeeds on the basis of their beneficial consequences, Gandhi asked himself. He did not have an immediate answer. Concluding that the question required closer examination, he walked on.

As he was crossing a famous road-junction in Delhi with the aid of his walking stick, a motor car broke through the mist and came to a halt near him. A police officer in a long overcoat and his driver, who wore two or three sweaters over his uniform, got down from the car.

'Sir, who are you? What are you doing here at this hour?' The policeman questioned Gandhi with an air of authority.

'Me? Gandhi. Mohandas Karamchand Gandhi.'

'See, it's started so early in the morning!' The driver laughed.

'We have no use for these stories, old man! Why are you loitering here at your age? You will freeze! Return quietly to your home. The trouble we go through because of people like you…! Do you think you can give them the slip if you wander around in disguise? They will shoot you, sir, they have guns, which are real.'

How can this man be so ignorant, Gandhi wondered. However, since he is an authorized representative of the government, it is my duty as an Indian citizen to answer any question he may ask, Gandhi told himself.

'I am not afraid of death, sir! If death should come to me in this manner, I will be happy. In truth, I am going now in search of death. Just half an hour ago, I left Birla House without informing anyone and set out on my own. I had no plan in my mind. But now I am thinking of going to Meerut. If I can find a railway station nearby…'

'Well, this seems to be a totally advanced case!' The driver started laughing again. 'It's so advanced that it can't be cured.'

The police officer became very angry.

'Old man, I'll advise you to stop prattling. Go home quietly. Else, if you really wish to die, go and die somewhere else…! Look over there. If you turn right at that lamp-post and walk through the narrow alley on the left, you will reach a small railway station. Nobody can say when the train will arrive. If, as you say, you are going to look for death, go there and wait. If a train comes by, that's entirely your good luck! But don't loiter here aimlessly. This is a neighbourhood where the country's most important citizens live. Can't say who will pass by this way and at what hour. We are engaged in providing security for the Mahatma, and we are having a hard time coping with everything. As if this were not enough, along come people like you!'

'I have told Nehru and Patel many times not to make any special security arrangements for my sake.'

When he heard Gandhi's remorseful reply, the police officer's eyes turned red. On seeing that his superior was really angry, the driver swung into action. 'Old man, are you going to clear off or not?' Brandishing his cane, he tried to chase Gandhi away.

Both men were in a fix, not knowing how to handle this crazy old man who was watching the driver's antics with an intrepid air and a rueful smile.

When they find out in the morning, they'll start looking for him. Dhaniklal will be the first one to announce it to the world, thought Gandhi. Then the enquiries will begin. Everyone will be grilled. All moving vehicles will be subject to inspection. They will easily guess that his destination is Meerut. He must get down on the way there. Gandhi hoped that God would have marked some obscure station between Delhi and Meerut as his Astapovo.

By the time he reached the railway station after walking through several narrow alleys, it had grown bitterly cold. On the smoke-filled platform, hundreds of travellers, their bodies swathed in rags, wandered around with their belongings. From their sleep-addled eyes and smelly bodies, Gandhi guessed that they might have been waiting there, assailed by hunger and thirst, for many days now. A babble of words in several languages – Hindi, Urdu, Bangla and Gujarati – collided against and bounced off the smoke-blackened walls of the station. Hundreds of grey pigeons could be seen sitting on the grills and railings. All of them appeared identical, as if they had been made up to look that way.

No one paid him any attention. But as he walked up the steps of the overhead bridge, a girl stared at him in wonder. She called out to her mother who was busy talking to someone else, and said something to her, pointing to him. Her mother looked up at Gandhi and then turned her face away in disdain. Gandhi felt an urge to speak to them.

He had to buy himself a ticket first.

'Are there any trains now to go to Meerut?' The question drew a derisive look from the man inside the ticketing booth, who pursed his lips and announced gloomily: 'No train is scheduled to depart from here anytime soon, for the simple reason that no train has arrived here for the past three days. That's the situation. You can see it, can't you? All these people are waiting here to catch different trains. We are tirelessly issuing all the tickets in our possession. These people, too, are waiting here with no signs of fatigue. The train has to arrive – that's all. Oh yes, where do you have to go? To Meerut? Or to Ahmedabad? You said Meerut, didn't you?'

'In fact, I don't have a definite plan. I think I will get on the first train that comes in.'

'That's a well known pattern, isn't it? That's what all your people prefer, right? They fasten themselves to any train that comes in first. However, not one of them buys a ticket. The ticket collectors, too, don't take any action against them. This can last only a few more days. The Sardar's hands are tied right now. They are waiting for it to happen. They restrain themselves on his account. Let it happen. It will be fun to watch what follows next!'

'Sir, forgive me. I don't understand what you are saying. If you can explain…'

The ticket clerk burst into loud laughter.

'Oh god! Let go of me, Bapuji! I can't keep explaining

everything. There is a train coming in. It will go upto Amritsar, trudging ever so slowly. Jallianwala Bagh is somewhere near Amritsar, isn't it? Have you been there before? Isn't it sacred ground for you people? You don't even need a ticket. Anyway, your people never buy tickets. Only for a few more days, until it happens.'

It was a matter of surprise to Gandhi that everyone was so informal.

'Give me a ticket to Amritsar,' he said, extending a one-rupee note.

'To Jallianwala Bagh, then?'

'Yes…! It's been such a long time since my last visit!' said Gandhi, smiling compassionately at the ticket clerk. Then the ticket clerk met the Mahatma's eye, and suddenly, his heart was filled with dread.

When he saw the five or six Gandhis who were pushing and jostling their way into a crowded compartment on the train to Amritsar, Gandhi was astonished; he hurried towards them, running part of the way. The crowd was huge and unmanageable. All those who were waiting tried to get into the compartment at the same time. Everyone tried to drag the others off the train in order to climb aboard themselves. Some even resorted to physical assaults. The entire railway station echoed with abuses and cries for help.

Gandhi stood diffidently near the door. But the crowd was growing bigger by the minute. He thought he might not be able to board the train. Fortunately, the crowd pushed him involuntarily into the compartment. Inside, he found that passengers numbering four to five times the compartment's holding capacity were packed into it.

Without any effort on their part, everyone had been pushed by the crowd to some part of the compartment. Gandhi felt depressed. His knees were aching intolerably. The train began to move. 'Here, Gandhi sir, come this way! Here's a bit of room for you! He looks really old. Give him a little room, the poor man. In spite of everything, he is one of us, isn't he?'

The clutch of Gandhis who had grabbed some space on a side-berth invited him to sit next to them.

'He seems to have come from far away! What might be your good name, sir?'

Looking in wonder at each one of them, all made up to look exactly like him, the Mahatma replied: 'Gandhi. Mohandas Karamchand Gandhi…'

They broke into loud guffaws.

'That we all know, don't we? I was asking your real name – the name your parents gave you …'

'It was my parents who gave me this name.'

'Your native place is Porbandar, then?'

'Yes, that's where I was born. Now, for the past few months, I have had to stay in Birla House. I walked out of there early this morning. Though I didn't have any plan when I left, now I am travelling to Amritsar. It's my wish to visit Jallianwala Bagh. It's been a long time since I last saw it.'

'It seems like a nut has come loose in his brain!'

'That's how much you know. In fact, this old man is smart. These days, fascination for such places has grown tremendously. Large crowds of tourists visit them every day. All you need to do is to put on this disguise and hang around there, doing nothing. You can earn more than enough money within a month.'

Unable to bear his disgust, the Mahatma closed his eyes. So this is how it's all turned out. Bhagwaticharan was not a lone man. The police officials he had met early that morning, the ticket clerk at the railway station and the pathetic people present in that compartment must have come across innumerable counterfeit Gandhis.

'But, Gandhi sir, please don't imagine that like you we have put on this makeup in order to beg on the streets,' said a middle-aged Gandhi in a tone of admonition.

'This man here, he is a Gujarati. A big landlord, he was in the Congress party for many years. He has even been to jail once. Only after we got Independence did he put on this disguise. He has still not met the real Gandhi. But his speech, gait and bearing are as striking as the real Gandhi's!'

'If he has no intention of begging, then why put on this disguise?' asked the Mahatma, his voice shaking.

'That's a good question. Our man has decided to contest elections. Sir, there is no easier way to ensure your win! Shave off your head. Wrap a piece of khaddar around your shoulders and waist. Hold a brand-new copy of the Bhagavad Gita in your hand. Then, step onto the street and keep walking. Like him, you must also walk at a brisk pace...!'

The more Gandhi heard, the more surprised he was. The man seemed to revel in what he was saying. As he was not quite past middle age, he must have made strenuous efforts to appear old. He had a slight paunch, and in order to hide it, he kept his stomach drawn in all the time. But he had no teeth. He might have had them pulled out in order to fit the disguise perfectly.

'Is it possible to earn the trust of people through such gimmicks?' asked the Mahatma, genuinely puzzled.

'This serves simply to draw people's attention. To straighten out your enemies and bring them around, you have to employ other strategies.'

'Only through non-violent means, I hope?' Gandhi asked him, looking at the man expectantly.

'Non-violent means? What a yarn!' he replied, accompanied by a belly laugh. Then he confided in a low whisper, as if it were a secret: 'Just a few more days! Let the event come to pass. Then I will become like Maharana Pratap. My men will chase them over and beyond the Himalayas. But Gandhi sir, you should go and beg on the streets, take care of your survival! Why are you wasting your time, listening to all these stories?'

The Mahatma started thinking about his own Astapovo.

The train stopped tirelessly at every single station on the way and started again. Despite travelling all day, it could not have covered even half the distance to its destination. The rush at the time of boarding had subsided totally. Four or five stops after Delhi, the clutch of Gandhis took their leave. But a fresh bunch of them got on board at every stop. Spectacles, khaddar and a copy of the Gita in one hand – the disguise is indeed very easy to assume, thought the Mahatma. Each man had his own reasons for wearing the disguise. The Mahatma noticed that there were several others who had also made themselves up to look like him. A young fruit vendor told him that this disguise helped them to escape from the rioters and the police.

'Even if the disguise is obvious, there is no problem. They think it would be a sin to kill someone who is wearing it. If I hadn't put it on, I would have been killed along with my parents when our settlement was set ablaze last month,' he told Gandhi. 'This disguise comes in handy even in selling fruit. Isn't it special to buy an orange from a mahatma rather than from an ordinary fruit vendor?' asked the young man, laughing.

Gandhi bought a couple of bananas from the youth and ate them. Then he lay down on an empty berth, stretching his legs. His body felt hot. Was it a symptom of pneumonia? They must be nearing Astapovo!

The dew began to fall as early as two o'clock that afternoon. To keep warm, one of the Gandhis sitting directly opposite the Mahatma began to smoke. Another gave up his disguise temporarily and put on a long, woollen overcoat.

Darkness had already begun to fall when the train halted at a very small station shortly after Panipat. Gandhi saw about twenty policemen leap aboard the third class compartment in which he was travelling. He imagined he was as good as caught. Immediately after they received the information in the morning, they must have swung into action.

The police held each passenger at gunpoint and grilled him.

Gandhi decided not to submit to any type of coercion. He must not change his decision even if Nehru or Patel came personally to plead with him. He scanned the platform to check if he had a visitor. The platform was deserted and empty. The station master could be seen in his worn-out uniform. After furling his flags and tucking them under his arm, the station master inspected the compartments one by one.

'What is your name?' Gandhi felt that he had seen the police officer somewhere.

'Gandhi. Mohandas Karamchand Gandhi.'

'Where are you coming from?'

'From Delhi…'

'Where are you going?'

'To Amritsar. I plan to visit Jallianwala Bagh.'

'Why are you going there?'

'It's been a long time since my last visit.'

'Show me your belongings.'

'But I haven't brought anything with me! I am carrying only a little money in a knot in my dhoti, money I earned with my spinning wheel. Apart from that, I have an old copy of the Gita with me, sir.'

The police officer asked Gandhi to untie the knot in his dhoti and show him the money; then he left.

To the Mahatma, it was hugely disappointing. There were only about a dozen passengers in the compartment. It had become completely disfigured by waste and rubbish strewn all over. The spaces underneath the seats were filled with several kinds of fruit peels and the remains of food. When he said that it was their collective duty to keep the compartment clean, other passengers laughed at him. In the afternoon, Gandhi started cleaning the compartment on his own. When he returned to his seat after sweeping up the rubbish and throwing it out, his fellow passengers threw coins at his feet. He gathered them silently and put them away inside the knot in his dhoti. By now the Gandhis, too, were disfigured beyond recognition. Their makeup had come undone. On the shaven faces of the young Gandhis, black stubble had begun to sprout. The usual hour for the Mahatma's prayers was approaching. A passing peanut vendor told them that it could take a very long time for the train to depart.

Have I reached Astapovo?

Thinking that he would walk for a while, he got off the train and set out alone.

Birds at the station were singing their nesting hour melodies. Nervously flapping their wings, they became agitated on seeing Gandhi. He walked away from there, not wanting to disturb their solitude. He imagined that he had finally arrived at a place where no one paid him any mind. This was a freedom he had never experienced before! Seated on a bench coated with bird droppings, Gandhi commenced his prayers in the dim light of a lamp-post.

'Why are you sitting here, sir? Are you a passenger?'

When he saw the station master standing before him, Gandhi tried to get up. 'Yes. I must get to Amritsar. I heard that it would take a long time for the train to start, so I came here to say my prayers. Do you have any information on when it might depart, sir?'

'No. I don't know. It is unlikely that anyone else would know either. We have received a message saying they've torn up the tracks.' After saying this, the station master looked oddly at Gandhi. 'So you are going to Amritsar? Do you have a ticket?'

It seemed to Gandhi that the station master, whose natural instinct was to smile, was making a strenuous effort at pretending to be strict with him.

'Here.' The Mahatma untied the knot in his dhoti and gave him the ticket. The station master moved a couple of feet away and examined it. When he looked up at the Mahatma, who had followed and stood near him, he was alarmed.

'Sir, what is your name? Please tell me.'

He spoke the truth, as always: 'Mohandas Karamchand Gandhi.'

Anxiety shone on the station master's face as he looked intently at Gandhi.

'Bapuji, please forgive me. I'll be right back. I need to examine this.' He hurried away with the ticket in hand.

It is most likely that I've come to the right place, thought the Mahatma. Suddenly, his body began to shiver. He was assailed by a fatigue he had never experienced before. He felt an unbearable pain in his joints. This seems to be the right time in the right place, he told himself.

His eyesight dimmed suddenly. Feeling weak, he sat down on the cement bench. Hasn't the station master finished his scrutiny yet? He thought catching a nap might make him feel better. He shook out his upper garment and covered himself with it as he lay down, folding his legs. The train which had brought him here stood motionless before him, like a corpse. If you left out the station master's small room a short distance away and the lamp-post, the place was really a jungle. The birds were crying incessantly.

A large bird perched at the top of the lamp-post with its black wings open was peering at him. This must be the bird which is going to announce my death to the world, thought Gandhi.

Dhaniklal will be the first to reach the spot. He may bring Manu along with him. I must leave my final statement with her, the Mahatma decided.

How wonderful it would be to have Ba here at this moment! Katurba had never fully understood the meaning of his statements. But there was no one who understood his silences as well as she did. Ba particularly liked Mondays when he undertook a vow of silence. It was on Mondays that she got the opportunity to stay with him all day, never leaving his side even for a moment. If she were with him, he wouldn't even need to make a final statement, thought the Mahatma. For him, her death was an irreparable loss. His eyes brimmed with tears.

'Bapuji, please get up. Your train is leaving. Bapuji… Bapuji! God, what will I do now? There is nobody here to help. Bapuji, Bapuji! O God…!'

The Mahatma heard the station master's agitated voice and the long toots of the train's whistle. He could not open his eyes. His consciousness was precarious, hanging by a slender thread. Whose train is this? Where is it starting from? Where is it heading to? Whose voice is this? Where are these sounds coming from? Is it Kastur's voice? Or of the little bird that lives on top of the tall red cedar tree? Else, are these the cries of the black-winged bird perched at the top of this lamp-post?

The Mahatma tried to open his eyes. He could not bid the world goodbye without making a statement, could he?

After covering Gandhi with a blanket, the station master ran with his green lamp, raising its flame on the trot, to see off the train which was about to depart for Amritsar. Shortly after, when he brought Gandhi some hot water he had prepared especially for him, he found that the Mahatma had sat up. On seeing the station master, the Mahatma gave him a toothless smile.

'Your train has left, Bapuji. You may have to wait another eighteen hours for the next train to Amritsar.'

The Mahatma sighed. Fortified by a sip of hot water, he was able now to get up and sit properly.

'Thank you. This seems to be God's wish. If he has readied this spot as my Astapovo, I could not go past it so easily, could I?'

The station master's face had turned pale.

'Bapuji, please forgive me. Help me avoid the blame for such an unpardonable crime. There is no one here! You will have to make even your final statement only to me, Bapu. I don't think I have the strength to bear it. Forgive me. The train to Delhi will be here within the next one hour. Please return to Delhi. It is there that everything must come to pass.'

The Mahatma laughed at this.

'Everything is decided, then! But, please tell me something. You recognized me right at the very beginning – how did you do it? You would have seen lots and lots of Bapujis, right?'

The station master laughed.

'That's quite easy, Bapu. Not one among those countless Bapujis ever bought a ticket. On being questioned, they would say, I got you freedom, isn't that enough? They would be spoiling for a fight. Besides…'

The Mahatma intervened. 'Besides, you had anticipated all this, hadn't you? You knew in advance about my journey and its objective!'

The station master grew agitated. 'But, Bapuji, please listen to what I have to say. It must not end like this. This should never be your message to the world!'

The Mahatma raised his index finger to silence him. Then he continued: 'No, my dear brother, I cannot retreat now. I have made my choice. I believe firmly, brother, that this world will understand the rationale behind my departure from Delhi and my arrival here. But, aren't there any doctors around here? Pneumonia has begun its virulent attack!' He lay down again.

'No, Bapuji. Nobody around here knows the first thing about pneumonia. Please agree to my request. Everything should happen only in Delhi,' he said and glanced at his wristwatch. 'God, only ten minutes left for the train to come. There's little I can do before that.' After mumbling to himself, he said to Gandhi, 'You must have reckoned this more clearly than anyone else, Bapuji. You must have walked out of there not with a wish to die, but with a desire to live. Your departure was intended solely to draw attention and elicit obedience, just like all the fasts you had undertaken earlier.'

As if he had no response to offer, Gandhi remained silent.

'But now, all your adversaries will see this from a different angle, Bapu. They have made up their minds. Yesterday or the day before, they might have faced defeat. But now, they have started their war against you. Today or tomorrow. Tomorrow or the day after… it's only a matter of days now.'

'What you are saying is true. But where did it all go wrong? I've been thinking only about this for the past three days! I considered every man my brother. Even those white men, who happened to be my enemies by dint of history, I loved them too. I tried to teach our people to do the same. I attempted to convey the message of truth and non-violence to everyone. In a way…' the Mahatma hesitated.

'In a way, you brought us the message of Christ! That's why the British Government could never kill you. You appeared to them not as a Christian but as Christ himself, Bapuji!'

'Yes, I am a true Christian; a Christian truer than Christians themselves.'

The Mahatma smiled. Talking to the station master was like talking to his own conscience. It was strange how his conscience was a station master in an obscure village.

'That's the reason our colonial rulers laid down their arms at your feet and left the country. They were unable to fight Christ, their god.'

'I am a Hindu. A true Hindu. Rama is my god. The Gita is my philosophy.'

'If someone accused you of having pulled off this deception, what would your reply be, Bapuji?'

Gandhi was silent.

'Tell me, Bapuji. From which sources did you formulate your precepts? From which god of our soil did you learn non-violence? Is there anyone among our gods who did not take up arms? Which of them forgave his enemies? On being asked to give away his shawl, which one gave away his dhoti as well? Who, on being slapped on one cheek, showed the other? Or, at the very least, did any of our gods follow the tenets of simplicity that you have urged everyone on to? Tell me, Bapuji…'

Gandhi heaved a deep sigh. 'What should I do as a satyagrahi? Please tell me, dear brother!' he said. Tears had formed in his eyes.

'Please go back, Bapuji,' pleaded the station master.

'No, that will be tantamount to death!' he said, repeating his teacher Tolstoy's famous sentence.

His conscience was angry now.

'Speak your own sentences, Bapu…! Face up to us in your own way. We are lying in wait to murder you. We have started this war to wreak vengeance on one another. We wish to settle accounts with history. The blood of a thousand years flowing on the streets of Delhi hasn't dried up yet. Teach us the nobility of your precepts or receive as gift the bullets discharged from our guns.'

The station master was gasping for breath.

'You will attain a poetic death, just as you wished, in the railway station of this remote village. Then we, your followers, will either betray you after your death or get killed. We will impersonate you even as we destroy your way of life. This sacred land is going to be filled with Bhagwaticharans. You will be ordained as God – merely a god who is powerless to change anything. Then, in the name of that god, a war of retribution will begin. It will last till your identity is completely erased.'

Both men fell silent.

The large black-winged bird, which was watching over Gandhi from the top of the lamp-post, intoned a cry of lamentation as it flew away. Its cry could be heard until it had traversed a long distance.

'Is this some kind of prophecy?'

'Prophecy or superstition – you can call it anything you like. But these things will come true, Bapu!'

Gandhi was absorbed in deep contemplation. He closed his eyes.

'No, I won't accept defeat. I will make my adversaries understand the poetic nature of non-violence!'

'Bapuji, then you must live out your entire lifespan – that is, one hundred and twenty-five years…'

The Mahatma closed his eyes and fell silent.

'Bapuji… the train to Delhi has arrived.'

Gandhi found himself a seat in an overcrowded third class compartment. He was merely another Gandhi among the several Gandhis travelling in the same compartment. The station master ran to him, panting, with a mug of goat's milk and a handful of groundnuts.

'You must stay well, Bapuji! Your death must be the message of our lives!' he said to the Mahatma as he wiped his streaming eyes.

Two days later, at three o'clock in the afternoon of 30 January 1948, the train in which Gandhi was travelling arrived in Delhi. When he reached Birla House on foot from the station, the time was fifty minutes past four.

Anxious that it was nearly time for his prayer meeting, the Mahatma entered Birla House hastily through the backdoor. In the mansion's expansive garden, Mahatma Bhagwaticharan sat looking at the burgeoning rose bushes. It is not known whether he noticed Gandhi's arrival. Gandhi hurried past him, turned into his room and entered the bathroom. He was washing his face when he heard Dhaniklal calling out to him.

'It's time for the prayer meeting, Bapuji! He is here.'

The Mahatma replied in a loud voice.

'I'll be there in a moment, Dhaniklalji. Please ask him to wait.'

Translated from the Tamil short story *Pirakoru Iravu* (2008).

Reversal

The clock's hands were revolving backwards, pushing time in the reverse direction. Just because she was a student of physics, she didn't have to see it as the backward journey of time. There must be a glitch in the clock's circuitry. There was no need to fret. Surely, there were other ways to tell time apart from looking at a clock? When Viswam apologized to her, the time was precisely six minutes and thirty-two seconds after eleven in the night. Most likely, his story too must have ended at the same instant.

She had looked at the clock only because she thought it was a very significant moment in her life. Making a mental note of the time, she went to the kitchen to make tea for Arun and herself. After tea, they went to the bathroom to wash their blood-splattered bodies. To them, it had only seemed like one of their usual moments. It required no effort on their part to forget, if only for the time being, everything that had happened earlier that evening. Neither Arun's sense of humour nor her playfulness was affected even slightly. Nor did they hesitate to exchange words dripping with love and desire. But later, Arun climaxed too soon, something they had never experienced before. She told him that it was only natural, that it might have happened because of the change in location – they were using the drawing room since Viswam's body was lying on the bed – but it failed to console him.

Then he set out in a hurry. Speaking in broken words and phrases, he urged her to be careful. He even promised that he would return as soon as possible. However, just as he was about to open the door and step out, he turned back nervously, as though he had left something behind, and bolted the door. She looked at him in confusion as she stood waiting near the door. Drawing close as if to kiss her, he told her in a whisper, 'Don't worry. I'll be back soon,' and instead of leaving, he walked quickly to their bedroom where Viswam's body lay. She followed him there. Standing only a foot away from the bed, he mumbled a few words at the corpse. Then he strode out of the room with the stiff movements of a soldier. She hurried after him. Pulling her close, he kissed her passionately, as if it might be their final kiss, and went out.

After washing her body, which was still moist from lovemaking, she stood in front of the mirror and started combing her dishevelled hair. The time by the clock was eighteen minutes and three seconds after eleven. That so much should have happened in no more than ten to twelve minutes surprised her. Deciding that the clock was certainly out of order, she focused on arranging her hair. It was then that she noticed that the clock's second-hand was moving backwards.

At first she felt confused and wondered whether it was an illusion. She looked at the clock again. The thin, red-tipped second-hand had completed one more backward revolution and returned to its original position. In step with its motion, the minute-hand slid back by a minute. Her blood froze. That was when the idea that time had reversed its motion took shape in her mind. Unable to recover from the shock of that notion, she kept staring vacantly at the face of the clock. She had collected herself, however, before the second-hand completed seven more revolutions in seven minutes. She had no time to lose herself in the giddiness of panic that was so typical of such situations. There were many things she had to get done.

The first task at hand was reckoning time. For telling the time of day, they had as many as three wristwatches and two cell phones besides the defective wall clock whose hands were now revolving backwards. But as if a cruel curse were coming true, she lost them all, one by one. On her first wedding anniversary, Viswam had bought her an expensive wrist watch. That apart, she owned another wrist watch, gifted to her by Arun seven months ago on her birthday. It was a tiny, ivory-coloured watch. To hide it from Viswam, she had stashed it in one of the seven compartments of a tin of assorted confectionaries in the kitchen. She never took it out when Viswam was at home. She wore it only after he left for work.

Viswam had stumbled upon it one day.

It was most likely the first thing that led him to discover her affair with Arun. During the row that ensued, unable to bear the ugliness of the abuses being hurled at her, she threw that symbol of their secret love out of the window. As though he was convinced that she had also jettisoned Arun's love along with that watch, Viswam calmed down immediately. He sat down on the sofa and unfurled the newspaper on his lap. It was the only way he could express his triumph over her, she thought. She yearned to hit back at him in some fashion. So she picked up the wrist watch that he had presented her on their wedding anniversary from on top of the television set. Viswam was foolishly expecting her to wear it. But suddenly she tossed it, just as she had done with Arun's wrist watch earlier, out of the same window. The watch fell from the third floor, cleaving the air with a whooshing sound, and struck the ground. He was shocked to hear the clear sound of the watch splintering. By the time she turned from the window to glare at him, Viswam's face had turned ashen.

She did not imagine he would drop the matter there. Curious for his reaction, she stood perfectly still, watching him. Then he looked up slowly. Pretending to be unmindful of her presence, he removed the watch from his wrist and examined it closely. It was a gift to him by her father on their wedding day. She guessed rightly that he intended to humiliate her by tossing it out of the window, just as she had done with his gift to her a few minutes earlier. However, she had to wait for more than ten minutes to see it happen. Precisely as she had anticipated, he tossed it out of the same window in the same manner, and then looked directly at her with vengeful eyes. She did not try to avoid his gaze. Instead, she faced his glare unblinkingly. Then, looking him in the eye, she smiled gently at him. That was enough to provoke him. Furious, he pounced on her, grabbed her by the hair, and struck a couple of blows on her back. Then he walked quickly out of the room. She could never forget that incident, which had occurred one evening six months ago, and now seemed to her like a melodramatic scene from a revenge drama.

After that incident, she used only her mobile phone for telling the time – to tell the time and to contact Arun. As if by some trick of destiny, she lost that phone as well during a fight on a different occasion.

While he was struggling earlier that evening to save himself from her and Arun, Viswam had used his mobile phone as a weapon of self-defence; now it lay broken underneath their bed. Before leaving, Arun had told her that they must get rid of Viswam's phone, too, along with his body. Arun, too, had a mobile phone, but when he left, he took it along with him, because she reminded him that he would need his phone for contacting people.

So, of all those devices for reckoning time, there was none left now. All that remained was a defective wall clock with hands that moved in the reverse direction, and a corpse which awaited removal.

Viswam was lying on his back on the bed. A post-graduate in history, he was also a leading criminal lawyer in the city. The man was prouder of being a scholar of history than a criminal lawyer, but his own history had ended now. Tomorrow or the day after, the bar council would surely pay tribute to the glories of his life. If only they knew that the city's leading criminal lawyer and scholar of history was killed by his own wife! But Arun would make it impossible for them ever to find out, by heaving that story into the black hole of time. If discovered later someday, the story would have decomposed so badly that even a post mortem might not be feasible.

The apartment was in a shambles. She tiptoed across the room, careful not to step on the shards of broken glass bottles on the floor, and reached the cupboard. The stench of death pervaded the room; only too natural, because a spanking new death had indeed occurred in there. It was doubtful whether even an hour or two had passed since then.

She couldn't come to a conclusion about what time it was, relying solely on a defective wall clock with hands that revolved in the opposite direction. However, she remembered that there were other ways to reckon time. Although time's journey was inverted, its motion was very precise nevertheless. Keeping a steady eye on the second-hand's backward revolution, she started snapping her fingers. This was a method she had been taught in school to calculate time. Precisely at the sixtieth snap, the minute hand slid back with a jerk, and the time on the clock was reduced by a minute. Every time the clock subtracted a minute from its time, she must add one more minute to actual time. All she had to do was to identify a correct moment that could serve as the reference point. Estimating the duration of each event that occurred after the last time she had looked at the clock could be of help.

Let's suppose they were engaged in certain activities after committing the murder – tea-drinking, for example. After tea, a person might spend five minutes to relax himself. Earlier, he would have taken five minutes to drink the tea. If we assume two minutes were used up before that to let the tea cool and six to eight minutes to prepare the tea, we may conclude that it would have taken twenty minutes at the most for a couple to have tea together. In this way, one must identify each activity and estimate its approximate duration. Even though the results won't be accurate, this method can be used whenever the clock is defective or, to be more precise, whenever we happen to see its hands moving strangely in the reverse direction.

Nothing major has happened here, except a murder and some tea-drinking, she thought. After successfully carrying out their plan, both of them had tea. She remembered their kissing. But was it before the murder and the tea? Their plan wasn't executed smoothly; they had to struggle a lot with Viswam. It was true that Viswam had remained inert till they put a noose around his neck, but he woke up as soon as the noose started to tighten. He became fully conscious in less than a minute and guessed immediately what was happening to him. He fought to save his life. He started railing against both of them using horrible obscenities. It made her even more violent. When someone hurls certain abuses at us, don't we become mindlessly brutal, without even being aware of it? For instance, a word such as 'whore' could make one spiteful. Only after she heard it did she grab the other end of the rope. When the rope snapped, it was she who brought the knife from the kitchen. Then she let loose a volley of abuses at him. She did not remember specifically the kind of swear-words she had used. 'Faggot! Who is a whore, now? You are calling me a whore? If I don't tear that mouth open, my name's not Sasi…' she would have said something on those lines. Because it was she who had slashed at and torn his cheeks open. Blood had spurted out and drenched her breasts. At that time, she might not have paid it sufficient attention. Later, when Arun grabbed and licked her, didn't he say that her breasts smelled of blood? Where did that happen – in the bathroom? No, as she was going from the bathroom to the bedroom, Arun had emerged from behind the bedroom door and embraced her. She even recalled her struggle to break free. But even in that terrible situation, something Arun had said must have prompted her to respond to his lust. Perhaps Arun had told her something like 'Sasi, please. Just once… This may turn out to be our last time. After tonight, it may not be possible for us to meet again.' She had a teacup in her hand then. Before that, she remembered going to the bathroom and washing herself in a hurry. But was it to wash away the blood from her body? And Arun was with her then, wasn't he? His clothes, too, were soaked in blood. Did he go out in those clothes? She had no means now to alert him about that.

Viswam's body lay in the same position as before, with his hands outstretched on either side. Blood was pouring out from his wide-open eyes. Perhaps it was the blood pouring out of his skull. Using a small hammer bought many moons ago for fixing nails, she had broken his skull. At that moment, he was kneeling at Arun's feet in a very disgraceful manner. 'Arun, if it's Sasi you want, please take her. Let me go, Arun… Please don't kill me, Arun,' he had cried, and babbled something else that was even more shameless, she remembered. She imagined that before dying, he was trying to meet her gaze directly. Later, when she accepted Arun's kisses and slid to the floor, Arun muttered that Viswam's eyes were watching them. Moving away from Arun, she tried to pull the lids down over Viswam's eyes, but they would not close. Arun, who was watching, came to her aid. Even after both of them tried shutting his eyes by turns, they could not succeed. Then she came up with a simple solution. Arun was surprised when he heard it first. Then he threw a towel over Viswam's face and got up. It was only later that they came to the drawing room.

For her, a student of physics, estimating the time taken up by each of these activities was not really a big challenge. All told, around an hour and a half. If the time was six minutes past eleven when Viswam apologized to her, now it must be at least thirty-five or forty minutes past twelve. But the clock seemed to be approximately an hour behind. If it had merely stopped running an hour earlier, there would have been no scope for confusion. But since its hands were curiously revolving backwards, different methods of calculation were required. But even this anomalous glitch in the clock's circuitry must be subject to some law of physics, she thought. Most likely, the clock must have changed its movement only after midnight. If that were so, the clock's hands, after moving along in the normal direction for fifty-four minutes after 11:06, must have started their reverse journey at 12:00 midnight. Now, the clock was twenty-five minutes into the reverse journey. From now on, it would not be difficult to compute the time. Every time the clock lost a minute, she had to add one. If the clock showed eleven thirty-three, the actual time was twenty-seven after twelve. It was very simple.

But that was not the first thing to worry about at the moment. They had to remove Viswam's body away from there within the next hour. But she couldn't arrive at a firm decision, given the uncertainty about when Arun might return. Some residents in her apartment complex, especially those who regularly went for a morning walk, would be awake by five or five-thirty. Maidservants, middle-aged housewives and hawkers selling fish and spinach would be up and about by then. It was imperative that they be done with the whole business before that, preferably between two and three in the morning. During that hour, the security guards went out to have tea at a bakery that stayed open for autorickshaw drivers under a flyover half a kilometre away. She didn't know if Arun realized he needed to be back within the next one hour.

She felt she was giving undue importance to such speculations and calculations. She forgot that she was a student of physics when she needed to, and remembered it when she didn't. She must put everything in order. She must restore everything to its former condition. Only the bedroom and the hall were in total disarray.

At one point, Viswam was able to free himself from them. He tried to smack Arun on the temple with a heavy object and escape. If they had not recovered in time, he would have pushed the door open and sprinted down the stairs. He could have even called the neighbours for help. She had reacted then with great presence of mind. Her eyes alighting on that hammer could have been fortuitous. Viswam had retrieved it for some purpose only two days earlier from under a pile of discarded household objects in the storeroom. After using it, he had dumped it on the table, and since then, it was being used as a paperweight.

However, the disruption in the kitchen took place after Viswam died. As Arun and she had the tea, she felt an uncontrollable anger towards Arun. She flung the teacup away and rushed to the kitchen, and leaning her back against the refrigerator, she sobbed her heart out. Arun followed her there and tried to calm her down. He caressed her hair, stroked her cheek and kissed the nape of her neck in an attempt to console her. She wept noisily. Then Arun touched her breasts. She resisted and broke free. She cursed him, grabbed a stainless steel vessel and tried to hit him with it. He managed to duck in time. She picked up another vessel and threw it at him. The kitchen was a mess in no time. Later, when they were making love, she said sorry.

It did not take her long to rinse the vessels and restore them to their former state. Wiping off the drops of blood that had splattered on the floor and walls was hard. Spotting them was harder, she thought. For instance, if someone were told that an ounce of blood had collected inside one of the kitchen blender's jars, would they believe it? But that had nothing really to do with Viswam.

It was around six in the evening. After grinding chutney, as she was trying to remove a bit of coconut kernel trapped in the bottom of blender, she was assaulted from behind by Viswam. Since he had grabbed her hair in a bunch, she could not do anything; nor could she withdraw her fingers without hurting them. If this had been discovered by television channels, they would have had a field day. She would have been portrayed as a vampire who churned her husband's blood in a blender and drank it up. Only after she had washed the blender and put it back in its place was she able to ponder the loss she had caused to the television channels by her act and how she had destroyed an item of evidence that her lawyer could have used to argue a plea of self-defence in case she was arrested.

She went to their bedroom where Viswam's body lay. Of all the rooms in the house, it had suffered the maximum damage. From the objects scattered on the floor, she picked up blood-stained items of clothing belonging to her, Viswam and Arun, and hid them in a plastic bag. After that, cleaning the room did not seem too difficult. Once she had neatly stacked the books scattered on the floor, the only thing left to do was to clean and arrange Viswam's body.

It was foolish of them to have thrown the books around, she thought. There were splotches of blood on several books. Some were so wet they could not be used any more. It was a big mistake to have placed the bookshelf right next to the bed, giving Viswam the chance to use the books, handy at his elbow, to assault them. The thick hardbound books served his purpose well. One day, when she was out, he had sold most of the shelf's contents by weight to a seller of used books. He had decided that it was reading those books over and over again which led her astray. In their fight over those books, she had heaped terrible insults on him. His manager, who arrived as an emissary of peace, had not only condemned Viswam's act in the harshest terms but also made him apologize to her.

She had scoured all the second-hand bookstores in the city in search of those books. Though she was able to procure some of them in newer editions, others had gone out of print. They appeared two months later in a used-books shop on the pavement in Mylapore. Like a story, she described to the shopkeeper how her books had ended up in his shop. Although he was sympathetic, he refused to part with them. He told her that they had passed through several hands before coming into his possession and that he had fixed a fair price for each book. He also agreed to give her a ten percent discount on the quoted price.

Without another word, she gave him the amount he was asking for, put all of them into an auto rickshaw and came home. Now most of those books had to be consigned to flames. Or, as per their plan, they would have to drop those books into the Cooum river along with their blood-soaked clothes.

After packing up the books and clothes separately in plastic bags, she looked around the room. Water bottles, tins of cosmetics, the mirror on the dresser (cracked when it fell to the floor, but with the shards luckily still within the frame), the iron, remote control of the TV and the monkey figurines placed on top of the television – everything was strewn helter-skelter all over the room. Since none of the items was usable any more, she dumped them all into a polythene bag. Now only the bed and Viswam's body lying on it were left. Once he was removed from the bed, she could change the sheets. Should she wait till the body was removed? She felt confused. She had no idea how the people with Arun were going to transport Viswam away from there, where they planned to take him, and what they intended to do with his body.

She had no doubt that Arun would have planned everything meticulously. When he arrived the previous night, he had brought a few jute sacks and polythene bags with him. He also brought a roll of nylon rope several metres long and a briefcase with an array of sharp knives. At first, she had thought that it contained liquor bottles. It was only natural for her to think that they might need the company of liquor to execute their plan smoothly. When she asked Arun whether they were going to use a knife to kill Viswam, he denied it with a vehement shake of the head. She didn't ask him anything further.

Regardless of whatever might happen, leaving the room in this state would be uncivilized, she thought. With some effort, even the blood-soaked bedspread could be changed. Given enough time, even the body could be wiped and cleaned. That would help the henchmen, who were expected shortly, to finish their jobs quickly and without any stress. To do this all by yourself, you needed, far more than courage, the technical ingenuity of an engineer, she thought. She felt thirsty. She carried a bottle containing lime juice from the refrigerator along with a glass to the bedroom and sat on the bed.

Viswam's body was beginning to give out a repulsive stench. It was not the smell of blood but the stink of faeces leaking out from his torn intestine. Taking the bottle with her, she entered the now spotless kitchen, sat on a polymer chair, and drank up the lemon juice in two large swigs. Then she covered her nose and mouth with a towel, tying it tightly around her face. Fetching a bottle each of Phenyl and Dettol from the bathroom cupboard, she returned to the bed.

Rigor mortis was beginning to set in. She could not fold back Viswam's arms and legs from their outstretched position. However much she tried, she could not even turn his neck straight. Without worrying too much about it, she used a towel soaked in a solution of Dettol mixed with water to wipe and scrub Viswam's entire body. Blood was still dripping from the wounds in his head and in the nape of his neck. She knew she had to stanch the flow. Luckily she remembered that there was a first-aid box, not used since ages, in the storeroom. In it she found, in not too damaged a condition, ten metres' length of gauze, a cotton roll, tincture of iodine and strips of Band-Aid. They would not be sufficient for her purpose, so she tore one of her cotton saris into several strips. She also collected the cans of eau de cologne that Arun had procured with forethought. The experience she had gained from her association with a voluntary organization providing healthcare services came in handy. She cleaned up each wound, packed them with strips of her cotton sari till the bleeding stopped, and dressed the wound neatly, using a piece of gauze and Band-Aid strips. After eau de cologne had been sprayed generously on each wound, the odour of blood subsided to some extent. Finally, she sprayed some air freshener to make the room smell fragrant.

Then the most marvellous idea occurred to her. From the drawing room, she brought a few vases filled with plastic flowers and placed them in the most suitable spots in the bedroom. Then she picked two brand-new dog figurines from the showcase and placed them on top of the television set facing each other. The apartment seemed to have regained its old sheen. She was even able to take pride in it. Then, she opened their wardrobe and selected a set of clothes that she thought fitted Viswam best. Since the rigidity of his body had begun to subside by then, dressing him was not too difficult for her. She straightened his dishevelled hair and combed it neatly. She rubbed cream on his face, now grown dark and gaunt, and added a thick layer of powder. Then she folded his hands as he normally kept them while sleeping, left arm across his stomach and right arm folded and tucked under his head. She did not fail to mutter to herself, 'Just like a child still,' as she habitually did, seeing him sleep that way. When she climbed down from the bed and looked at him from two feet away, she felt very satisfied with the result of her efforts.

She imagined that anyone who saw him now would only think that he was fast asleep. To her, he appeared more handsome now than ever before. The room, filled with the fragrance of eau de cologne, looked as finely decorated as one decked up for a wedding night. She felt that she alone – standing there looking unkempt, with her body reeking of blood – did not belong in that room. She took out one of Viswam's favourite saris with sunflowers on a dark blue base, and went into the shower. She returned with only a towel wrapped around her. She even felt a little shy while changing clothes. As she walked gently, mincing her steps towards the bed, her cheeks turned red. She found it unbelievable that she should blush so. Sitting with her back resting on one of Viswam's outstretched thighs, she ran her fingers over his hairy chest, gazing steadily at him. She remembered old times. How many times had she sat here and looked at him exactly this way. She was startled out of her reverie when her eyes fell on a red-yellowish liquid trickling out of his nostrils. Perturbed by the sight, she took the small wad of cotton left in the first-aid box, rolled it into two little balls and closed up his nostrils with them.

His body was decomposing; it was rotting inside. Whatever happened to Arun? Where was her secret lover who had promised to be back as soon as possible? What if he was unable to return? What if the kiss he had given her before he took leave was their last? What if he had left her to flounder in this ruined apartment, saddled with this rotting corpse? She became agitated. She became aware of her body losing control over itself and shaking involuntarily. Afraid that she might collapse to the floor, she held on to one of Viswam's hands for support, the hand of a decomposing corpse that awaited men to dispose of it. But incredibly, holding that hand consoled her. She reckoned it was only a few minutes since Arun had left. He could not have reached even the outskirts by now. He had told her, and she, too, didn't think it would be easy for him to find the right people for the job. Perhaps it was the defective clock that was stressing her out so; her sense of time had gone awry. Hunger and sleeplessness were other factors.

She thought she would recover from weakness and nerves if she drank a little fruit juice or tea. When she opened the refrigerator, wondering whether there would be anything left, she was surprised to see among its neatly stacked shelves, which showed no signs of disruption, a sealed bottle of lime juice.

Staying alert was very important. She recognized that instead of losing her way in useless fantasies about the past, she must think up other ways out of her situation. What if she, all by herself, cut up this rotting corpse into little pieces using the knives from Arun's briefcase, stuffed them into polythene bags and jute sacks, hired a taxi, and with the driver's help, threw the packages one by one in different spots all over the city? Or, she could transport Viswam like a patient in an ambulance, drive to a remote place, douse his body with petrol and burn it? Even in her highly-strung mood, she didn't believe that finding a taxi or an ambulance driver, who would consent to all this and keep their secret, was such an easy task. She wondered if she could abandon everything in the apartment as it was, with its defacements and rank odours, and escape to a zone where it was impossible to get caught.

Or she could tell a story, a story so common these days that anyone would believe it. At midnight, a few bandits laid siege to their isolated apartment, attempted to rob their money and jewellery, and assaulted the couple, who tried to stop them and raise an alarm, with hammers and other deadly weapons. The husband's skull was smashed. There was blood everywhere. In the struggle to protect herself, she rushed pell-mell around the apartment. Their bedroom and kitchen were turned upside down. Even after throwing fat books and heavy vessels at them, she was unable to cause any kind of injury to even one of them. Supposing one, or all four who had barged in, subjected her to sexual violence? No. Claiming that one man alone dragged her to the kitchen and raped her, or the robbers merely assaulted and robbed them and then got away, would do. Then she fainted and collapsed to the floor. She regained consciousness only in the morning. She entered the bedroom to check on her husband. Viswam's corpse was lying, blood-soaked and disfigured, on the bed.

She could not decide if this story fitted her context and sounded plausible. She was surprised that even after drinking an entire bottle of lemon juice her body hadn't cooled down. She kept pacing up and down till she was totally exhausted.

Then, as if she remembered it suddenly, she looked at the defective wall clock. The minutes were ticking by. Time kept moving in the reverse direction at a steady pace: from thirteen to twelve, twelve to eleven, then to ten, nine, eight, seven, six, five, four, three, two and one; finally, to nothing.

She was frightened. Her body's heat kept on rising to intolerable levels. She wished she had some fruit juice left in the bottle. She reproached herself for having consumed every drop, without any forethought. When she opened the door of the refrigerator to check if there was anything else that she could drink, she was jolted to find another brand-new bottle of lime juice. 'God!' she cried out, shocked. She slammed the door shut and collapsed against it in great fear. The refrigerator, no more than four-feet tall, shook. Low, moan-like sounds were emanating from it. She felt she was being hurled into an unreal, mysterious zone. Suddenly, she sensed a sweet fragrance pervading the air. What was this smell and where was it coming from?

She drew the air deep into her lungs and tried to identify the fragrance. Wasn't this the smell of the air freshener they had been using for a long time? She was surprised that she had not been able to identify it right away. On second thoughts, it wasn't surprising at all. Because the air freshener was sprayed somewhat excessively, it had smelled a little different to her. But she cheered up on seeing that the house was more spick-and-span than ever before. Spotless and spanking new. The vessels were stacked neatly. Floor, walls, racks and bolsters – every nook and corner of the apartment glittered as though it had been finished and opened for use just moments earlier.

She then came to the drawing room. Although it looked clean and new, she noticed that a few things were amiss in the drawing room. The flower vases were missing. A crumpled pillow lay untidily on the sofa. Shocked to see one of her undergarments hanging obscenely from the arm of a polymer chair, she grabbed it and threw it into the laundry basket. Then she straightened the crumpled pillow and carried it to the bedroom. As soon as she entered the bedroom, she noticed the flower vases. 'Yes, of course, I totally forgot,' she whispered to herself. The smell of eau de cologne in the bedroom turned her stomach. That mixed with the smell of Dettol would fade away if she sprayed a little more air freshener, she muttered to herself and looked for the can. Instead of its usual place in the cupboard, it was lying on the edge of a bookshelf. This lack of order was not something she could be proud of. When she knelt on the bed to retrieve it, she had to disturb Viswam who was lying across her path. 'You haven't got up yet? Do you know what time it is, Viswam?' she asked, while glancing at the clock whose hands were revolving in the opposite direction.

However, it was not the defective clock alone that served to remind her of the present and its fraught moments. As she looked from Viswam's body, which was beginning to give off a stench, to that finely appointed room pervaded by the fragrance of eau de cologne, to the clock which was pushing time in the opposite direction, she realized finally that she could never return to the past. It would be nothing less than foolish to believe any more that Arun would come back as promised. There would be no opportunity to tell the 'story' she had cooked up. She had foolishly ruined everything herself. Without any time left to make new plans or implement them, she had no option but to surrender herself to the morrow. The student of physics stood helpless, having completely lost control over time.

In two more hours, before the minute-hand completed one hundred and twenty revolutions in the reverse direction, tomorrow's account would have commenced. The corpse would begin to rot and stink. Handcuffs awaited the strange wife who killed her husband, dressed up his body and then sat watching over it. Some other subsequent 'tomorrow' would close the account of her life, and reduce her to nothing. For her, tomorrow would be totally empty, without light, without hope. In fact, from now on, there was no tomorrow for her; all that remained was yesterdays: yesterday, the day before, and the previous thirty-one years. Perhaps time itself was rushing backwards in search of yesterdays. The hands on that clock – were they pushing time back as they revolved? Had the laws of motion of the universe inverted themselves?

If only this weren't the frenzied imagination of a student of physics who had teamed up with her secret lover and killed her husband, but was now clueless about how to get rid of the body, and had been abandoned by her lover who had gone away, promising to return.

So, life was going to travel not towards tomorrow, but back towards yesterday; and from yesterday to the day before, and all the yesterdays that came before. From now on, there was no tomorrow for her, for any living thing. We only had yesterdays. Whatever happened yesterday would be what happened tomorrow. Life day after tomorrow would be the life lived day before yesterday. In this way, in the days and months and years and aeons to come, the history of mankind was going to travel backwards.

How was man going to face this erratic motion of time which had embarked on a reverse journey towards the past? Why would it interest him to traverse those abandoned paths again? Could it even be called a journey? What if everything that had come to pass should happen again, this time in a reverse sequence? If that came true, the future would have no room at all for riddles and mysteries. No room for dreams either. The achievements of mankind, which were essentially the fruit of dreams, would not be needed in the future – or, more precisely, in the past. Time had shut its door on man, deciding what he knew so far was enough. Man, who traversed many aeons searching for what he did not know, had to now get by on what he already knew, hang upside down like a bat on time's branches and eke out his living. The life that man had abandoned as obsolete, thrown away as useless, he had no other option but to retrieve and safeguard that very life, unmindful of the repugnance he felt for its deformities. No help for it until death arrived!

Recalling the word 'death' gave her a jolt. She felt more drained than before. If only there was a little more juice left!

By chance, in the course of time's backward journey, what if the lime juice had returned to its original state, its ingredients separated into mere water, sugar and limes, and each of them had in turn begun to journey backwards? She would no longer be able to drink the juice of that particular lime, she thought. As time passed in reverse order, subtracting constantly from its account, at some point that lime might return to its tree. From ripe to green to tender, and then to flower, its journey would be retrograde. The flower would turn to bud, and bud to sprout. What after that? After that, it would no longer have any shape. Its journey would end as a void in time's black hole.

In fact, there would be no scope from that moment onwards for something like death; only resurrection would take place. All living beings were going to journey towards the moment of their birth. Each life that had embraced death and lay buried, reduced to nothing, was going to awaken at some instant. Bodies ravaged by age and disease were going to rise from graves and ash-heaps. All life was once again going to suffer the cruel pains of old age and disease. Each being was going to live once again, but along a reverse trajectory from old age to infancy. The end would no longer be a passage into the grave but an entry into the womb. Even there, nine more months of living awaited each being. And it could be prolonged for a few more days or moments, half in the mother's ovum and the other half in the father's sperm.

Then…?

Then, nothing. The end would be the same as death, from the void to the void. She was disgusted at this continuity of life's unchanging pattern, which endured regardless of the direction of time's movement. She checked carefully whether there was any sign of life in Viswam's body. What if he turned over suddenly at some point? What if he was able to wake up, raise his hands over his head and stretch them in an attempt to shake off languor? She, too, could travel back to her childhood, couldn't she? First, as a teenager; then, as a child. Both phases of her life had been full of joy. Even her life with Viswam had been joyful until a couple of years ago. What if she could get back the torrid moments of his lust, his love? In that case, this glitch that had developed in time's motion would indeed be worth celebrating.

There was a little juice left in the refrigerator. She swallowed it in one gulp and then went to the bathroom and washed her face. She placed a polymer chair next to Viswam's bed and sat there gazing at him. There was still time. Exactly eleven minutes and seven seconds were left. When that tiny second-hand reached, on its reverse journey, the precise moment when Viswam had asked for her forgiveness and embraced death, he would wake up. She asked herself if she would apologize to him when he woke up. She felt confused. She wondered if the old rancours and fierce love would still survive in a man after he came back to life. Sasi wanted to lose herself in fantasies about what life would be like with a man who harboured neither hatred nor love in his heart.

A sudden moan from somewhere flustered her. She leapt up from the polymer chair. Her body trembled. She began to perspire profusely. She gingerly approached Viswam's body and, with trembling hands, removed the sheet and looked at his face. Viswam's nostrils appeared bloated to her. One of the cotton balls she had stuffed into them a short while ago had rolled out and now lay on the nape of his neck. She even felt that his ribcage was rising and falling very gently. Placing the back of her hand below his nostrils, she checked for breath.

But there is still some time left, isn't there? Exactly five minutes and nineteen seconds.

Her heart began to beat at an incredible rate. She abruptly moved away from his side. What would Viswam do when he came alive again? Would he know that he was Viswam? Would he be able to remember her, know who she was? What would he remember of Arun and her relationship with him? Of the rancours past, fissures formed, abuses exchanged and quarrels that flared up between them, which ones would have remained alive in the recesses of his memory? Which ones were likely to rise to the surface and continue? What if Arun returned before that happened? What if he came back with people to assist them in getting rid of Viswam's body and rang the bell? God, how horrible it was, being the first witness to time's reversal of its trajectory. From where was she going to derive the strength to face such horror?

Could she escape this crisis? What if she ran away somewhere? What if she fled to a place uninhabited by anyone and lived out the rest of her days? But... what did 'the rest of her life' mean in the face of time that had reversed its course?

She rose from her chair. Opening the wardrobe, she took out some clothes. After stuffing them into a tote bag, she started out in a hurry. Let the consequences of his resurrection be whatever they may turn out to be. What I must do right now is to flee from the pain of confrontation, she thought. When she came to the drawing room from the bedroom to look for her slippers, she saw a crumpled pillow lying on the sofa and her undergarment hanging obscenely from the arm of a polymer chair. But hadn't she, only a short while ago, thrown that undergarment into the laundry basket? She also recalled having carried the pillow to the bedroom.

It was then that the flower vases struck her eye. She clearly remembered taking them to the bedroom after Arun left. Time was indeed travelling in the reverse direction. Everything that had happened earlier was happening now in the reverse order. Every object was returning to its original place.

As she flung her bag away and entered the bedroom, her face turned ashen with terror. Their bedroom was in a mess, exactly as it had been earlier. Books and water bottles were strewn all over the room. Blood had splattered and congealed on everything – walls, windows, cupboards, table and chair. The room was filled with the smell of a very recent death. She could smell neither the eau de cologne nor Dettol. She concluded that the room must have looked exactly like this a few minutes after Viswam had pleaded forgiveness with her and his life was snuffed out.

Exactly two minutes from now, that very moment would arrive. Racked by anguish at having to be a direct witness to Viswam's resurrection, she sat next to him on the bed. She leaned on his shoulder and bent forward, as if to kiss him. She unblinkingly watched the face of that cadaver from which all blood had drained out. The second-hand on the clock kept revolving in the reverse direction, pushing time towards the past. Only sixty seconds were left. Just one minute. But Viswam's body lay stone-like, without the slightest movement, showing no sign of the impending resurrection. She was growing impatient. She waited, snapping her fingers in time with the backward movement of the second-hand. Forty, thirty-nine, thirty-eight, thirty-seven... What if everything turned out to be just a figment of her imagination?

But there was no need to lose hope. She would hold on till the final moment. It could happen in a second. One second does not always mean a trifling measure of time. Sometimes, a second can turn everything upside down. A year ago, when Arun declared his love for her, she took no more than a second to respond.

Translated from the Tamil short story *Olikkum Piragu Irulukkum Appaal* (2009).

Victim

She looked extremely frightened and perturbed. Huddling close to the wall like a kitten, she glanced fearfully around the room. The air was thick with the stale smell of sweat.

Bolting the door shut, he pulled her close, forced his mouth on her lips and kissed her roughly. He squeezed her voluptuous breasts.

She sighed.

Then she shuddered, as if to communicate her lack of consent. Perhaps because she had not co-operated as expected, he let go of her. Taking off his trousers and shirt, he wrapped a lungi around his waist. Feelings of rage and annoyance, natural at such moments, showed clearly on his face.

Reclining on the bed, he lit a cigarette looking steadily at her all this while. She was still standing in the same spot, her head lowered to avoid his direct gaze.

He could call her to bed. He knew the words to use in such situations, and what he had to do if they didn't produce the desired effect.

He kept smoking cigarette after cigarette, as if trying to smoke away the inexorable lag between idea and action.

His gaze closed in on her. The hum of the fluorescent lamp reminded them of the fearful silence pervading the room and the streets outside, both steeped in melancholy.

She waited tensely for that terrible moment when the silence would break. He might have taken her silence, too, as an insult. 'Like two pathetic characters in a horrible pantomime' is how the narrator describes them.

The brothel-keeper had not lied to him. The girl was new to the profession. It was only a couple of days since she had been brought here, the brothel-keeper had told him. He was happy that he had not been taken for a ride.

Experienced sex workers would know how to conduct themselves in such situations. Sometimes, just to retain the customer and induce him to tip them generously, they behaved in disgusting ways. They took off all their clothes the moment they entered the room. They remained completely naked during the few hours they spent there. Some drank with him. Experienced readers would know that I am not lying, says the narrator.

That none of them did such things with any degree of involvement, he understood after only a few days of visiting prostitutes. But he could not find adequate reasons for discontinuing his visits.

Even now, he felt no pity for her. He tried to think of ways to make her yield without forcing her. At least, the narrator thinks so.

She was a real beauty, with a very fair complexion and a childlike face that was totally unsuitable for this profession. The splendor of her virginity had not been spoilt yet. She must be a reward for a loyal customer like me, he thought.

In that case, he wouldn't have an easy time of it; he might have to force himself on her. This was something he was not used to. Even supposing that he dared to, there was every chance that she would scream and shout, or break into loud wails.

The way she stood there, it was certain that she was about to break down and cry any moment. And if she did, it would be the cry of an abandoned child – God, how would he bear it?

I am caught in a really terrible predicament, he thought. He was not used to such dilemmas. He wondered whether he should get out of there immediately, take her back to the brothel-keeper and extricate himself.

But he realized that this was an absurd idea. What he had failed to do here, or not wished to do, another customer might do far more cruelly than he could ever have. No doubt, that was precisely what would happen during the remaining hours of that night.

The reader might ask whether it is possible for a person like him to think on those lines in such a situation, the narrator presumes. There is no categorical explanation for such things, and the answer might lie in the enigmatic recesses of the human mind, replies the narrator, almost evasively.

If I allow her, actually help her, to escape, she will be quite willing to get away, he thought. That might put him in a spot. The brothel-keeper would be angry with him. She would demand a large sum as compensation. He wondered whether going to all that trouble for the sake of someone who was still a complete stranger was really called for.

When he saw her standing there like an ancient sculpture whose lustre had dimmed, stricken by an indescribable sorrow, he felt despondent. He decided to help her regardless of the consequences, but he scarcely knew how to convey this intention to her. Since he had no proper words to broach the subject with her, he felt humiliated in a way.

Should he call her, give her some money and tell her, 'Look here, girl. I can't tolerate your living a whore's life. Get away from here and go somewhere else.'

Should he advise her to work towards a decent life? How

would she respond? Would she agree, thank him and go away? Would she, greatly moved by this completely unexpected succour, start crying? Or, what if she suddenly burst into laughter?

Really, the chances of that happening could not be ruled out.

Anyway, she would definitely have a story. Like running away from home, naively trusting a lover's promises or propelled by movie ambitions – a story of the times.

He called her.

She looked up in surprise and stared at him. The evident compassion in his voice was unbelievable. She stood still, wondering whether the voice had been a figment of her own imagination. But he called her again. Pointing to a chair near him, he told her solicitously to come and sit there. She smiled like a child, delight spreading over her face. As though she had read and understood all the pages of his mind in that single invitation, she came forward with a spring in her step and stood next to the chair.

Asked whether he likes to create characters with noble traits, the narrator denies it vehemently. If you and I were in these characters' shoes, we would have behaved more or less in the same fashion; it is inevitable, says the narrator.

'Sit…'

She looked diffidently at him.

'Sit…' he told her again in an almost pleading tone. He wondered if he should offer her anything to eat. He remembered that he had a few biscuits, a packet of chips and some coffee in a flask. He got up, fetched the items from the cupboard and offered them to her.

'Eat…'

She looked at him, frightened.

'It's all right. Eat…'

He drew up another chair and sat close to her, like a friend. To ease her shyness, he took a biscuit himself and bit into it.

Her fear assuaged, but still shy, she began to eat.

He felt happy. Now she wouldn't refuse his help, he imagined. He was surprised that he could be so kind to anyone. By then, she had started eating very fast. He realized that she was very hungry.

He asked her what her name was.

She answered as she continued to eat.

'Nice name.'

He told her what was usually said on such occasions. Then he asked where she came from. She stopped eating and looked at him with dismay. He became nervous. He was afraid that their conversation might not continue further. He told her in an apologetic tone that he had simply wanted to know and that she didn't have to tell him if she didn't want to. However, after drinking a little water, she did tell him what he wanted to know. Her confidence in him fluttered in her eyes like a butterfly's wings. Like a ripe brown leaf dropping to the ground, her words emerged quietly and without fuss.

'...'

He was shocked. He couldn't believe it. He wondered if she was lying. But it was easy to tell from her face that she was not a liar.

She was from his native village.

His kith and kin still lived there. He had tried to forget that village and the demeaning past he had left behind. Now it was back like a nightmare in the shape of this girl. It was a completely unexpected, cruel coincidence. Feeling upset, he struggled to find his bearing. He could give her a little money, or as much as she needed, and send her away.

Impelled by a powerful, involuntary urge, he began to speak.

'There…' he struggled. He was out of breath.

'Which family do you belong to?'

She looked at him in confusion.

'Tell me, whose daughter are you?' he asked in a threatening, peremptory tone.

After a long silence and a bitter sigh, she said, 'A man called ___________, he is my grandfather.'

'Him!' He nearly shouted. The name hit and smashed the burial pit of a wretched past that he was trying to forget. 'He is your grandfather? Him?' He began to whimper like an ill person, a madman. 'This is totally incredible, one of life's perverse games,' is the narrator's comment on this development.

Hers was an orthodox Brahmin family which had once been very affluent. Her grandfather had walked majestically in the dark streets of the village as though he was God's own messenger. His father and grandfather had regularly cleaned the shit-filled trench in their house. He had breathed the odour of shit from his mother's womb. The stomach-turning stink of shit, born before all of them and sure to live on after them, sat arrogantly inside their low huts like an omnipotent spy who had the power to monitor their dreams and destroy them in their foetal state. She sat before him like a corpse resurrected from the grave of his memory.

'Have you heard about the family of ______?' he asked, mentioning his grandfather's name. His voice was full of hatred. His hands were trembling. Drops of sweat broke out on his forehead and on the back of his neck.

'No,' she replied in a low whisper. Suddenly, her childlike gaze turned sharp. She looked searchingly at his face, as though she was trying to find some trace of his forefathers in it.

'He had cleaned the latrines of your forefathers!' he told her angrily.

'Yes, I remember,' she mumbled in fright. On the curtain of her memory, a dim, foggy face appeared momentarily.

'He is my grandfather…!' he shouted with joy. 'He cleaned your latrines. He and my father – in fact, all my forefathers did only that for a living.'

She had turned pale as a corpse. Like someone who had lost her faculty of speech and had nothing to say, she looked at him with tranquil eyes. Enraged, he blew white smoke from his cigarette on the girl. Like a faithful hunting dog, the smoke from his cigarette laid siege to her. As if it was there only to keep an eye on their activities, silence sat cross-legged between them.

But it is hard to explain the moment when that silence broke. Even the narrator does not know which of the two had created a fissure in the intolerable silence that hung in the air between them. The narrator expresses regret at having to tell this tale. Apart from apologizing for his failure to observe the events precisely, he also asks defiantly how he could be faulted for not being able to relate this incident like a story. As he continues, the narrative with his angry expression and trembling voice, we feel both pity and contempt for him at the same time. But he does narrate what is most essential from everything that needs to be said.

'Whore! Why haven't you taken off your clothes yet?' He shouted angrily at her, and she – merely submitting to his anger or deciding that a prostitute's duty was to satisfy the customer's every whim and of her own accord or impelled by some other reason – took off all her clothes and made herself naked, the narrator does not fail to tell the readers.

'I am going to fuck you,' he told her, his voice quavering.

'I am a whore!' After saying this in a firm, clear voice, she walked calmly over to the bed and lay down on her back. He fell on her, inert as a corpse. There was no lust in his breath. He grabbed her like she was prey and held her roughly.

'I'm an untouchable,' he whispered spitefully in her ear.

'I'm a whore.'

'My father picked up your shit.'

'I'm a whore.'

He told her after spitting saliva into her mouth:

'We eat the flesh of dead cattle.'

'I'm a whore.' She swallowed his saliva.

Pushing her aside, he got up and shouted angrily:

'You were born from Bramha's head…'

'I'm a whore,' she said in a limp voice.

She was using that word as a shield to protect herself and also as a weapon to attack him, says the narrator.

'You're a whore,' he spat on the floor with revulsion. This time, she did not reply with 'I am a whore'. It was the answer to all the questions he had asked so far as well as the ones he was going to ask. As if to say that the answer had already been given, she stared at him with listless eyes.

'I will give you ten times the money we had agreed on.'

Her eyes widened in surprise.

'Maybe I'll give you a hundred times… yes, a hundred times more money, maybe.'

After this firm announcement, he opened the bureau, grabbed all the money inside and threw it at her. He searched all over the room like a madman for coins strewn randomly on the window sills, in the gaps between bookshelves and in shirt pockets…

In truth, I would like to stop the narrative here, says the narrator. Even though he may attract criticism for stopping abruptly, he can avoid the spiritual tension that would result from continuing the story, he says. But he can also think differently. Perhaps he lacks the necessary courage: he is perhaps afraid that his story will be ruthlessly attacked by critics for being the product of a vulgar, bestial and perverse imagination, for being opposed to our traditional culture and humane ideas. Or the remainder of the story might be unacceptable even to the narrator. As with the confession of a convict subjected to indictments and humiliation, the narrator tries to speak in a subdued voice.

As if he would like to show his reader that in reality or fiction, in some part or nearly every part of the world, there have been incidents, actual and imaginary, comparable to or far more terrible than this one, our narrator draws quotations from news reports, post-war novels in French and German, Latin American short stories, poems from Africa, films by famous film-makers who were expelled from the Soviet Union, why, even Roman plays and Indian epics, and tells the rest of the story through these sources.

In fact, this is an amazingly adroit move. It might help not only the narrator, but also the readers, to escape from what the narrator has called 'spiritual tension'.

As in novels and films, everything happened at demonic speed. He tied her hands and feet to the bed, stuffed her mouth with a piece of cloth, sat naked in front of her on a chair, lit a cigarette and drew the smoke deep into his lungs till the fire at the tip of the cigarette was wholly red and came to resemble the vengeful eye of a predatory animal, then calmly pressed the cigarette's burning end into all possible spots on her naked body. All such deeds of his as well as her agony as a result of this unbearable torture, and her screams which ricocheted against the walls of her ribcage and died away, bore a precise resemblance to the stories and films that he had quoted from.

If the narrator so desires, the story can be wound up at this stage. But he says there is much more that remains to be said. It is no longer under his control; the story is moving along hesitantly towards an independent denouement, the narrator says. He requests the reader not to interrupt him.

'You wouldn't know about it. Outside the village, on slushy ground filled with shit… the place looked like a model for hell…,' he started telling her in an agitated voice, as if recalling a nightmare. Her eyes wanted to say something to him.

'That was where we lived,' he said angrily as he blew out cigarette smoke. 'Like pigs… even our breath was considered untouchable. My grandfather has told me of those barbaric times. We walked with mud-bowls hanging from our necks. Because your scriptures decreed that since we ate the meat of dead animals, even our spit would sully the earth, we walked around carrying those symbols of slavery like begging bowls.'

In her eyes, there was atonement beyond the torment of cigarette burns.

'Those scriptures were written by your ancestors,' he whispered vengefully in her ear.

'We are born to work like cattle in your fields and clean your latrine pits. Ha…! We have to quell our hunger eating the stale rice defiled by your spit, it seems. We have to hide our nakedness with your discarded rags. Our women wander around half-naked like whores…. even today!'

He trembled. Tears struggled to break out from the depths of his heart. She was saddened to hear his tear-drenched words.

'They called us sons of whores. Our women stood before your men with their breasts bared.'

She wanted to scream. Tears flowed from her eyes and streamed down her cheeks.

'Every time we refuse to accept any of this humiliation, we are attacked.'

The walls of the room shouted along with him, and echoed as though endorsing his words.

'You call yourself noble souls and boast that you were just to the cow and the dove. When our children jumped into your well, didn't you electrocute them? For demanding an extra quarter measure of paddy, you threw our women, children and youth into a fire and burnt them alive! You put out the eyes of our people! How will you atone for these crimes? Where is your justice?'

She cried like someone returning a favour. She wept for the cruelties inflicted by her grandfather and her ancestors on him and his forefathers. As if atoning for all those cruelties, her body was charred all over. She wept as if she had sacrificed herself for him, without protest…

The narrator stops there. He smiles as though he has just recounted a funny story. Like quizzing children immediately after telling them a story, he would like to put some questions to the reader. What a strange man!

Well, he wants the reader to guess how this story will end. Or, what kind of end would you like, he asks of the reader.

He advances certain possibilities.

The man kills the girl in the end; or she dies on her own from extreme torture or excessive mental agony. In case both these endings are not to your taste, he understands at some stage what her tears mean, realizes his guilt and releases her; or, as it often happens in movies and novels, he announces that he is going to marry her as atonement for his deeds and moves the reader; or, as it happens in mystery novels, the police or a few social activists break down the door and enter the room to find the girl in a critically injured condition…

But you are laughing!

Even the narrator finds these arguments laughable and juvenile, it seems. Nevertheless, under such circumstances, on those lines, unavoidably…

So, for the narrator, this too is a story like any other story, isn't it?

Translated from the Tamil short story *Bali* (1993).

Ruin

Agaligai sat leaning against the wall, her hair loose and in disarray. She was weeping. I thought she would kill me somehow. Some of her motives were general; some were special – that is all. I don't think I need to explain them to you. If you're still eager to find out what they are, I'll think you are an uncivilized voyeur with a shameless urge to watch your neighbour having sex. Please forgive me. I don't have the time to argue with you.

Oh God, my wife is about to kill me, no doubt about that. She is going to slit my throat with a knife or plunge the knife into my chest and cleave my heart. Of the two, she'd much rather slit my throat, because the sight of blood spurting out of it will make her feel ecstatic as in an orgasm during intercourse. Only if she can't, for some reason, do it this way, would she choose the second method. But she won't do it any other way. She can easily smother me with a pillow on my face when I am asleep or mix poison in my food. But she'll do neither. Blood gushing out of my slit throat; my headless torso writhing in a pool of blood; my head, with unblinking eyes like in an antique sculpture, rolling on the floor; the crowd of people gathered to gape at the spectacle; stinging words of abuse adrift in the wind; and Agaligai, standing proud with her bloodstained hands in shackles, a defiant stare in her flaming eyes… what a wonderful scene!

Agaligai called me to dinner. I got up calmly and followed her. We didn't speak to each other during the meal. But when we were about to finish eating, Agaligai noticed my perplexed expression and the beads of sweat on my face.

'What happened?'

I didn't reply, for she might have guessed that I was already aware of her plan to kill me.

'Are you ill?'

'Y-y-y… yes.'

'What is it?'

'I have a slight fever and headache.'

She came to me and placed a hand on my forehead. Then she brought her hand to my neck, pretended to check my temperature with the back of her palm, and felt the left side of my chest with her fingers.

I felt my pulse quicken. My heart was pounding fast, as though it was about to jump out of my rib cage. Breathing became difficult.

The fruit knife was lying at the far right corner of the dining table. From where she was standing, Agaligai could, without removing her left hand from my neck, pick up the knife with her right and, in the blink of an eye, plunge it in my throat; or she could hold me down and stick the knife into my chest.

'Wait. I'll heat some water. You'll be all right once you've had an aspirin.'

I sighed with relief.

Unable to sleep, I stayed awake all night. Agaligai lay fast asleep beside me. She was really in a deep slumber and not feigning it. It must have been post-coital exhaustion.

I got up gingerly, like a cat. I picked up the flashlight from under my pillow. I also turned off the bedroom lamp which was spreading a soft blue light in the room. Careful to avoid making any noise by scraping my feet on the floor, I tiptoed my way to the kitchen.

The knife still lay on the dining table, exactly where I had seen it earlier. I examined it under the beam of the flashlight. It was not sharp like I had imagined. The wooden handle was worn out. The blade had blackened over time and its edge was blunt.

I used the attached clasps to secure the flashlight to the edge of the table. Then I laid my left thumb on the tabletop and, holding the knife comfortably in my right hand, pressed and drew the knife's edge on my finger. It pained where the knife had touched the finger, but there was no wound, just a line where the knife had pressed into the flesh. I fetched a banana, laid it on the table and drew the knife along its length. Under the knife's pressure, the pulp broke and burst through the skin. Then I tried to cut through a head of cabbage, a beet and a potato. I found it really hard to slice them. During this exercise, the knife blade hit the surface of the table repeatedly, making a series of taps. Whenever that happened, the sound drove me to panic. I had to turn off the flashlight immediately, stand completely still and watch for any signs that Agaligai had woken up, before I could resume my trials. I opened the window and threw the sliced bits of vegetable and fruit in the gutter. Then I searched the room carefully. She could have hidden another new and shiny knife somewhere, couldn't she? As best as I could, I looked carefully in all the likely places – the wooden cupboard where the utensils were stacked, inside the vessels, and in the tins filled with grocery items. But because of my haste, fear and nervousness, I was unable to conduct a thorough search.

Keeping my roiling heart under control, I returned to the bed and lay down quietly.

Only when Agaligai woke me up in the morning with a cup of coffee did I realize that I had fallen asleep.

'Do you still have a headache?'

'No,' I replied quickly.

When I stood in front of the mirror after brushing my teeth and washing my face, my own face looked frightening to me. My eyelids were swollen. Tiny capillaries had spread their branches across the white expanse of my eyeballs. There was a faint black ring around both my eyes. Out of a sense of precaution that Agaligai not notice my facial changes, I was very mindful of all my activities. Even while we ate, I made sure that the straight line of her gaze did not alight on my face. Fortunately, both of us were in a hurry to get to work. I dropped Agaligai at her office and then reached mine. I felt totally restive at work. The howls of wolves hunting corpses in a cremation ground ricocheted against the walls of my brain and raised echoes. I handed in a leave letter and came home directly. After latching the door from inside, I walked into the bedroom and collapsed in the armchair. I lit a cigarette and began to reflect on my situation.

I closed my eyes, trying to retain a picture of Agaligai in my mind. I saw a shape resembling Agaligai, but it was faceless. Instead of a face, a triangular glass prism glittered in its place. That glass prism laughed at me. It was a demon's laughter. Even as she was laughing, Agaligai vanished in a plume of smoke. There was a flood of smoke everywhere. White smoke as from a cigarette rose in a chain of rings. Agaligai's naked body appeared through the curtain of smoke. Hers was the quintessential kind of voluptuous, virginal beauty; the magnificent splendor of femininity. I couldn't open my eyes. My mind was transfixed by her image. Agaligai looked at me and laughed – a mystic laugh that set my heart on fire. I knelt before her.

Agaligai held out her hands in the air.

A knife that shone like a piece of the sun materialized from somewhere. With a cruel laugh, Agaligai hacked one of her fecund breasts, bursting with the vitality of youth, and threw it away. Laughing relentlessly, she severed and threw away the other breast too. Blood spurted out of the gashes where the knife had cut through. Her dancing picked up speed. She seemed to be dancing to an inaudible melody without missing a beat. Miming a dance movement, she bent down and cut the flesh of her thighs with the knife and scooped it out. Then she deftly sliced the flesh off her buttocks, shoulders, back, belly, calves and vagina, and threw it all away. Severed arteries gyrated all over her body. Her dancing had reached the peak of its frenzy. Her laughter resounded like thunder.

When the burning end of the cigarette touched my finger, I came back to my senses and opened my eyes. Smoke from the cigarette crawled upwards in a straight line in front of my face and dissolved into the air.

I got up, went to the bathroom and washed my face. I drank a glass of cold lime juice from the refrigerator. Then I looked at the clock. There were at least five hours left for Agaligai's return. Before she comes home, I must search the entire house and find the knife she has hidden away, I told myself.

I began my search calmly and carefully, without undue excitement. I started with our bedroom, a space common to both of us. I stroked the mattress and pillows to check if my hand pressed on something that felt suspicious. I checked everywhere: drawers in her cupboard, her neatly folded clothes, suitcases, different kinds of leather bags. I couldn't find the knife in the hall either. Although the kitchen had been searched earlier, I checked there one more time, slowly, taking my time, but was disappointed. Failing to find the knife after two thorough searches in the space of two-and-half hours, I felt dispirited. I was also irritated with myself.

In order to calm the turbulence and clamour of my mind

until Agaligai's return in the evening, I kept pacing up and down the house. The soles of my feet became sore and my aching legs began to tire and collapse. As soon as the door bell rang, I opened the door with the air of having returned home just moments ago and then started walking back to the bedroom.

'You seem to have come back early from office today.'

The gentle patter of Agaligai's footsteps behind me scared the hell out of me. She could be carrying the knife in her handbag, couldn't she? I couldn't say for sure if I walked fast with the objective of escaping from her. But I was stopped by a wall. I turned around abruptly to face her and stood leaning against the wall.

Agaligai stood before me like a full-grown teak tree. Her gaze pierced me for a few seconds. Frightened, I raised my right leg to take a step back, but my heel grazed against the wall. Through the corners of my eyes, I looked at what lay to my left and right. Agaligai took a step towards me. When she throws the knife at me, I should slide down instantly, push myself between her legs, knock her down and get away from here, I calculated.

Agaligai came near me and placed the back of her palm on my neck and chest.

'How is the fever?'

'Well…it's better now.'

With my tongue cleaving to the roof of my mouth, I fumbled for words.

'It looks like the fever is gone, but why are your eyes so red?'

'….'

'Okay. Wait, I'll heat some water. Take another aspirin, and you'll be all right.'

After hanging her handbag on the coat stand, Agaligai went to the kitchen. I got busy immediately. I scrambled hastily to inspect the contents of her handbag. What bad luck! The knife was not in her bag either. Knots of confusion throbbed within my brain. A terrifying cacophony of sounds rose all around me. I collapsed head first on the bed with a thud. A storm was brewing in my world.

In the period that followed, gales blew in my mind daily, gathering speed and whirling madly. I began to understand that a whole lot of people – my colleagues, superior officers and subordinates who worked with me; fellow passengers, conductors and drivers whom I had befriended during my daily commute; and the rest of mankind (excluding me) – secretly carried a knife, wanting to kill me. How had I known them for so long without understanding their real nature? But I was glad that at least at this stage of my life I was able to grasp the truth.

Quite often, whenever I could spare the time, I came home early from the office, even taking leave on a few occasions, and ransacked the house for the knife. Although I couldn't find it, my state of alertness gave me a lot of satisfaction.

A remarkable incident occurred during that period.

At the invitation of a colleague in the office, I happened to visit the main shopping area of the city one evening. He said he wanted to buy a nail clipper. I was amazed when I looked at his fingernails. Each nail was sharp and glinting like a knife-blade.

We came to a small shop adjoining the pavement. I was overcome with depression. Attractive-looking knives, sharp and dazzling like the sun, were arranged tastefully. I asked the shopkeeper whether the knives were for sale. The shopkeeper laughed and said yes. His laughter struck me as insulting. Angry, I asked him why he was laughing.

'Don't be angry, sir. Surely, you must know that all goods in the shop are for sale?'

'Okay. Who buys these knives from you?'

'Who? Everyone, of course!'

'Does "everyone" include women and children?'

The shopkeeper replied thoughtfully, 'Children don't buy knives, obviously, but women…? So far, only one woman has bought a knife from me.'

I felt a mixture of thrill and excitement.

'Only one woman?'

'Yes. Just a lone girl,' he said emphatically.

'Who was she? Do you know her?'

I could see webs of confusion forming in my friend's eyes. The shopkeeper stuck out his lip.

'No. After all, I don't ask my customers any unnecessary questions. Forgive me.'

'All right. How old was the woman?'

'Around thirty.'

Oh, God! Agaligai, too, was about to turn thirty, wasn't she?

'Was she fair-skinned?'

'Yes.'

My pulse quickened and my face broke out in a sweat.

'Did she have a pepper-sized wart on her forehead?'

'No. Who are you? Why are you asking me these questions?'

'Please tell me. I need to know everything about this woman.'

'Forgive me… telling you anything more will be a breach of business ethics.'

I paused for moment.

'Okay. What kind of knife did the girl buy from you? At least tell me that.'

I was pleading, more or less, but the shopkeeper scrutinized me with his even more confused look.

'What do you mean by "what kind"? Please explain.'

'Would she be able to kill a man, specifically her husband, with that knife?'

'Yes,' he said, with apparent certainty.

'Okay. Let's go,' my friend gripped my shoulder. After carefully making a mental note of everything – the shop, shopkeeper, and the street on which it was situated – I followed my friend.

We entered an eatery and sat at a vacant table.

'Tell me,' my friend began.

'What?'

'Why did you behave like that? I don't think you are a mental patient.'

Without replying, I got up, went to the washbasin, washed my face and came back. I wiped my face with my handkerchief.

'Tell me,' he said again.

'What?'

'Why did you behave like that with the shopkeeper?' His gaze fell on my face as if to examine something there. After scrutinizing me from head to toe, he looked penetratingly into my eyes. Without trying to look away, I stared back directly into his eyes. My friend's face turned pale and fear-stricken. Without answering his question, I asked him, 'Do you wish to kill anyone?'

'No,' he replied, visibly alarmed. He looked frightened as he turned away from me.

'Why are you asking me?'

I ignored his question.

'All right. Do you expect someone to kill you?'

'No, why? Who would want to kill me?'

I could see that his body was trembling. He looked around fearfully, like a cat.

'Who is going to kill you, huh?' I couldn't control my laughter. Forgetting that it was a public place, I slapped the table repeatedly as I fell about laughing. Because my laughter had exceeded normal limits, I could feel my eyes welling up with tears.

'Please stop laughing,' pleaded my friend, his voice hoarse and cracked by now.

Abruptly, I stopped laughing and asked him in a harsh tone: 'Why are you acting like an innocent? Liar! You are such a fraud…'

'…'

'Tell me, do you think your wife won't kill you?'

Shocked, he pushed his chair back noisily and stood up.

'What are you saying?' he said in a hushed whisper. He must have actually wanted to shout at me, but he had not perhaps failed to notice that we were in a public place and that the attention of a lot of people was focused on us.

'What are you saying? There is no reason why my wife should want to murder me.'

He faced me with a weak smile. I could see that he was trying to pretend as though we were having a friendly argument.

I told him calmly: 'A wife has just as many reasons to kill her husband as not.'

After this conversation between us, he stopped interacting with me altogether. I did not worry too much about it, nor did I have the time for such concerns. Taking leave on the next day as well, I ransacked every inch of the house. But this time too, only disappointment awaited me.

That night, while we were making love, Agaligai asked me in a whisper: 'Do you remember what is special about tomorrow?'

In the dark cavern of my mind, there was a sudden flash of lightning. 'What's special about tomorrow?'

'You really don't know?'

Oh! Was tomorrow the day I had been waiting for? I held her tight and kissed her passionately.

'Tell me, what's special about tomorrow?

'It's our wedding anniversary. Don't tell me you forgot!'

My dear Agaligai! What a fine aesthetic sense you have! Murder your husband on the day of your wedding anniversary… Ha, ha, ha! My mind jumped for joy. The vision of fresh blood bubbling and flowing… after many days, I slept peacefully that night.

But towards dawn, I was troubled by a doubt. How could she kill me when she didn't have a knife? As soon as this question surfaced, my mind was once again rocked by confusion. Suddenly the face of the shopkeeper we had seen in the market appeared in my mind.

Ha…!

Run, run, run over there and buy it right now! What if Agaligai gets hold of the knife that would inflame her urge to kill you! Gautama, death is beckoning you! Run!

This time I was alone with the shopkeeper. He knew somehow that I would come again. He had chosen a knife especially for me, he said. He handed me a knife that glittered like a shard of lightning. I paid him twice the amount he asked for. Later, after I had thanked him and was about to leave, he asked me hesitantly: 'Could you tell me what you intend to do with this knife?'

'Sure. My wife needs a knife with which to kill me.'

The shopkeeper conveyed his greetings to me. I entered my house very carefully. Again, there was a thick drizzle of panic in my mind. Agaligai was in the bathroom. Aha, what a fine opportunity! Anyway, she has to come here after her bath to change, doesn't she? Quietly, I entered our bedroom. I took the knife, kissed it and, opening her wardrobe, placed the knife on the middle shelf so that it would be directly visible when she opened the wardrobe. Then I closed the wardrobe as before, came to our bed which was right next to it, closed my eyes and lay down on my back.

My life's final moments.

When Agaligai comes into the room after her shower and opens the wardrobe, her eyes will fall on the knife that's going to set off her murderous frenzy.

I tried to erase these thoughts from my mind.

But many thought-bubbles were foundering in the lower depths of my mind. As if the founts of greed within me had opened up suddenly, there was a gush of emotion; the steed of thought struggled to get up on its feet, then broke free of its reins and began to gallop, hooves pounding the dust.

The walls of my brain cells were juddering. The warmth of the morning sun; the unfolding petals of a rosebud; the lost face of one's first lover; a poem – any of these at random…

Oh, a soul's last wish!

Do I wish to say a prayer? Prayer? Prayer for whom? For me? For God? Do I believe in God? So far, I have neither abused nor worshipped God. How unfortunate! What, after all, is the point of a life which has never encountered such a question nor attained clarity on it?

Even now, I can get up in a jiffy and remove the knife, adorn her hair with the rose that's bloomed in my subconscious, share that poem with her. I imagine that I can even talk to her about my first love.

But it's too late now.

I hear the sound of Agaligai's footsteps, followed by the screech of hinges as she opens the cupboard with the knife inside!

Translated from the Tamil short story *Azhivu* (1989).

Staying Alive

Carrying their baskets and spades, Sadaiyan and his gang of friends reached the north pond of Pannadi woods.

Sadaiyan climbed into the pond and cast a quick glance around. The snakeheads and butterfish lying on the edge were alarmed and fled noisily. The mullets and catfish swam to and fro, their bellies up and bodies glinting like fireflies.

There wasn't much water in the pond, only wet and porous slush that rose up to the knees. No one had ever seen the ponds in Pannadi woods dry up like that. The rains had failed completely that year.

'Imagine, even the ponds in Pannadi woods dried up,' the people said, speaking of the drought.

'A robber's haul of fish is lying here in this pond. The mullets and herring here are this fat,' said Sadaiyan, holding his hands apart to the width of a thigh. At once, all their faces glowed with happiness.

'We'll drive all the fish beyond a line, erect a partition there and drain the water on the other side completely. Then we can stir up the mud and catch them easily,' said Sadaiyan.

Sadaiyan was like their leader. Not only was he the oldest among them, but he was also very adept at getting things done. He was the one who told them what to do and how to do it. They found that the job got done quickly if they followed his advice.

He was the one who usually found out and informed them about a particular job in a particular place. Even that afternoon's project was something he had discovered. Otherwise, the boys would only while away their time in the yard, sitting under the tamarind tree and playing a game of dice or draughts.

They cut a bundle of wild grass from the fallow land adjoining the canal bank and brought it to the pond. From the upper layer of the fallow terrain, they cut out mud slabs four fingers deep with their spades, and carried them to the pond to erect a barrier.

They had only three spades between them.

A group of three boys – Veeran, Pazhani and Thattaiyan – entered the pond, drove the fish to a corner and completed the task of erecting the barrier. Sadaiyan, Mottaiyan and Karuppan cut the mud slabs from the ground and brought them to the canal bank.

After erecting the barrier and reinforcing it with a coat of clay, Sadaiyan said, 'We four will bale out the water. The other two can stand on high ground and capture the fish. Make sure no fish escapes to the other side, into the water.'

'You have to be very alert. The moment you see a fish, just grab it…'

They baled out the water using the big basket lined all round with buffalo skin. Whenever they had to dig a well or drain out slush, they used this basket to bale out the mud.

Standing in that half of the pond with the fish in it, they baled out and flung the water on the far bank, on the other side of the barrier. The water flowed back later into the fishless half of the pond.

As time passed, the water level began to go down. As the water in the pond decreased, fish began to appear in the water. As the landed fish writhed on the ground, with reflected sunlight glinting on their silver bodies as though they were spawned by the sun, Sadaiyan shouted: 'Oye…! Don't just stand there feasting your eyes! The fish are pouring down here! Pick them up and put them in the basket!'

After the water level came down to the ankles, everyone entered the pond.

'Put your feet and hands in the mud and stir it up good and proper. Only when the mud is churned nicely will the fish come floating up,' said Sadaiyan.

Everyone rushed into the pond, shouting with excitement. They stirred the mud roughly. 'Ussaai!' they ululated. When the mud and water combined to form slush that was like a stew of cow dung, the fish rose to the surface with their mouths open. It was easy to catch these open-mouthed fish as they came up.

As the mud was stirred up more and more, plenty of fish rose to the surface. While only the mullets and catfish came up, the freshwater garfish, snakeheads and butterfish hid themselves in the mud.

'Everybody join together and stir it up, and the fish will be yours! You have to catch the butterfish and snakeheads by their heads. If you catch the body, they'll slip away. It's the same with garfish…'

The sun's heat was fierce and stinging.

Even at mid-day, no one left to eat. They had to walk a mile for just a little watery gruel of raagi, didn't they? By then, enough fish had been caught to fill a big basket. Sadaiyan insisted they catch another basketful somehow. They stirred the mud some more. Mud from the bottom of the pond rose up and filled the pond. Fish were swiftly captured.

When the others declared that the pond had been emptied out, Sadaiyan said: 'There is a big garfish left in there! Don't climb out, any of you! It's a rough beast.'

Eagerness showed instantly on all their faces.

They stirred up the slush even more vigorously. They foraged in the mud, specifically targeting the garfish mentioned by Sadaiyan. Sadaiyan, too, was involved in the intense hunt.

'Look properly. We can't let it slip. It's a real big one.' Sadaiyan's voice was cheering them on.

'Got it! Got it!'

Hearing Pazhani's exultant shout, everyone rushed to his side. Pazhani's hands were buried in the mud.

'What is it? Is it a garfish?'

'Yes, anna. It's a garfish.'

'Hold it carefully. I stumbled across this one in the beginning. It's a big, fat creature.'

Everyone held their breaths. Pazhani paddled his arms back and forth in the slush. 'It's biting me, anna.'

'It's biting?' Sadaiyan asked, surprised.

'Yes, anna. Sharp and stinging, like snakebite.'

Their faces froze in an expression of grave silence.

'How can there be a snake here?' shouted Sadaiyan, almost in a threatening tone.

'Garfish bite like that, can't do much about it,' he declared emphatically and continued: 'But it won't do any harm! Hold on to it! Grab its head! If you grab its head, push your fingers into its mouth and hold tight, even a big one will not budge an inch.'

'No, anna. It's biting,' said Pazhani in a pleading tone.

'All right. Let it go and climb out. What do you say, anna?' Veeran looked at Sadaiyan's face.

'Why, da? Won't you people just shut up? Pazhani, you hold on to it, don't let go.'

No one said anything. Pazhani's face was contorted in pain.

He was new to the task of catching fish. He had worked with them, digging wells, cutting trees and cutting cane. But he had never been with them on a fishing expedition. He was indeed happy that a big garfish had come into his hands. If he succeeded in landing it, he would be recognized by Sadaiyan as a keen lad. But the pain was intolerable. He bit hard into his lower lip, which started bleeding as his teeth sank deeper. Ignoring it, he struggled in the mud to hold on to the fish.

'What, Pazhani? Has it slipped away?'

'Will I let it slip? Now it's firmly in my hand. I am holding its head.'

'Is it a garfish, really?'

'Yes, yes. Garfish only.'

Everyone was staring at him without blinking an eye.

'It's ours! Can't get away!' Shouting, Pazhani stood up and ran towards the bank.

Everyone ran behind him. Pazhani reached the bank.

In his hands there was a long, rope-like garfish… No, it was a snake, a watersnake.

When someone shouted, 'Aiyo, snake!' a startled Pazhani threw it down. The snake, frightened and aggressive, leapt instantly into the pond and disappeared out of sight.

'A snake. Pazhani said right at the beginning.'

'If he did, he should have just choked it.'

'What if things had gone wrong? It isn't such a treasure, is it?'

'Like shaving off your moustache for a single night's stage performance…'

'Like honing the beak of a scavenging hen…'

'Say it, say it!'

Their voices besieged Sadaiyan in their fury.

'Won't you all just shut up! These idiots dare to open their mouths as if they know everything,' yelled an agitated Sadaiyan.

'Enda, Pazhani, can't you tell the difference between a snake and a fish? Here, show me where it's bitten you,' he drew out Pazhani's hands gently and examined them.

The backs of both palms, smeared with slush, were badly swollen. Sadaiyan's face creased into a frown and darkened. Pazhani screamed.

'Aiyayyo, Sadaiyappannaa. What do I do now?'

'Ei, don't shout. It was only a watersnake, not a venomous one.'

'It's paining, anna,' cried Pazhani plaintively, his eyes filling with tears.

'Yes, yes, it will pain all right. I'm not saying it won't. But there is no danger to your life from this snakebite. This was a watersnake.'

'Anna! Shall we go to the hospital, anna?' Pazhani's voice trembled. Tears pushed their way beyond his eyelids and tumbled out.

'Yes, even if we need to spend five or ten rupees, that's all right. Poor chap, he is the father of two girl children.' As Thattaiyan spoke, Sadaiyan felt a sharp stab of anger.

'Enda, won't you shut your gob and stay quiet for a minute? Can we afford to go to the hospital for every little thing? You think we own fields growing paddy?'

'Yes, those who talk – what do they stand to lose?'

'No, anna. Let's go to the hospital. The pain is killing me.'

'Look here… there's no need for all that. The spot where the snake bit you… all you have to do is to go there and drink three mouthfuls of water from the pond. Everything will be all right.'

'But that water is all mud and slush, anna!'

'What if it's slushy? As per the rite, three gulps. That's all.'

Dragging Pazhani along with him, Sadaiyan got into the pond again. The rest followed the two men.

When they came to the approximate spot where the snake had been caught, Sadaiyan said: 'Scoop up the water and drink three gulps.'

'It's all slushy, anna.'

'So what? If you are finicky, nothing will happen. You will be cured only if you drink this water. Just close your eyes and drink three gulps.'

Pazhani brought his lips close to the slush. As soon as his nose touched the murky water which reeked of rotting fish, his stomach turned. His face was contorted with anguish and revulsion. He struggled to stand upright. Sadaiyan did not let him. He put his hand on the nape of Pazhani's neck and thrust his face once again into the water.

'Anna. No, anna… listen to me. Let's go to the doctor, anna. It's very slushy, anna. Please listen to me, anna. Aiyo.'

With the force of Sadaiyan's hands, Pazhani's face was dipped in the slush. The mud entered his eyes and inflamed them. He gulped down a mouthful of slushy water. Overcome by revulsion, he lifted his head immediately. He felt nauseous and got ready to vomit.

'Tha, tha. Don't vomit, appa. Then your life itself will be in danger.'

One among the men who were watching came forward to assist Sadaiyan. Together they dunked Pashani once again in the mud.

'Just two more gulps, right? Close your eyes and drink up,' said Thattaiyan.

'No, anna. I've had a mouthful as per the rite, haven't I? Then why should I drink more?'

'Ei, what kind of man is this? He is behaving like a total lunatic! Tell him to drink three mouthfuls of water as per the rite, and he is telling us stories. Just dunk him in the mud, da,' Sadaiyan shouted in frustration. Another man joined them. All three pressed down on the nape of Pazhani's neck and made him bend down.

Visibly in distress, Pazhani swallowed another mouthful of muddy water.

'Enough, anna. I've had two mouthfuls, haven't I?'

'Enda, you have to drink three mouthfuls as per the rite, so just swallow one more,' said Sadaiyan as he hit Pazhani on the back of his neck.

'Anna...'

'Close your eyes and drink another dose, da, Pazhani.'

With great difficulty, he swallowed another gulp.

'So, what's happened to you now? What did you create such a commotion for?'

With Pazhani leaning on their arms for support, they brought him to high ground. Fetching water from the well in the garden, they washed his body. Fear hadn't quite left Pazhani.

Sadaiyan called Veeran and told him: 'Veera, take Pazhani home and leave him there. Inform his wife.'

'Yes, Anna,' said Veeran, as he walked away supporting an enfeebled Pazhani with his hands.

'Don't fall asleep, Pazhani. Tell his wife to heat a pot of water and let him catch the steam. He will be all right. What harm can that snake do, just a watersnake. At my age, do you know how many times I've been bitten by snakes?'

Veeran and Pazhani climbed up the canal bank and walked on. Pazhani tottered as he walked. Wordlessly, their companions watched them go away.

Sadaiyan yelled once again.

'Pazhani, don't go to sleep, da. You have to stay awake. Veera, tell his wife about this and come back. Tell her to heat a pot of water and give him the steam to inhale. After dropping him home, come to the north pond.'

It looked as though Veeran turned around and said something in reply. But in the roar of the wind, none of them could make out what he said.

Translated from the Tamil short story *Jeevitham* (1980).

Remains

Everyone treated him with affection. When they looked at him, they immediately arranged their faces to look affectionate. They regarded showing him affection as their duty. It was simply not done to withhold affection from a young man who had just lost his father.

Subramaniam sir recognized him even as he was getting down from the bus. 'Ada, is it you? Come, thambi. Are you doing all right? You've returned so suddenly; couldn't you have dropped us a line? Is everyone at your home doing fine? Has your mother gotten better? That little tyke… what's his name…? Your father was so fond of him.'

He nodded his head once in reply to all their queries and said: 'We are just fine, sir. Are you all doing well, sir?'

'We are getting by, thambi. Isn't it sad that our sir has passed away like this, in such an untimely fashion? But we can't brood over it and worry endlessly, can we? Don't we have to move on and see to everything that needs to get done?'

With memories of his father kindled within, he walked behind Subramaniam sir, tracing his footsteps. Subramaniam was indeed like a father, with a father's physique, voice and disposition.

'So you've come to collect your father's belongings?'

'Yes, sir. Appa's rented house has to be vacated, isn't it? Otherwise, there can't be a whole lot of his things here.'

'Yes, it's true. He only had a couple of vessels for making and drinking gruel, a few clothes to wear, a mat to sleep on and a blanket. Then there is an old bicycle left that he used to ride to school. Its tires and tubes are of no use. If you change them and do a bit of overhauling, you can use the cycle for a few more months.'

On their way to Subramaniam sir's house, they were spotted by Sangilimuthu sir and Dorairaj sir, who started walking along with them. All three men had done a lot for Appa during his final days.

On the day Appa died, he had sent a telegram to the headmaster. All the teachers travelled overnight and arrived at his house by morning. Subramaniam sir touched Appa's feet and wept like a small boy. Sangilimuthu sir and Dorairaj sir consoled everyone at home. 'Your father is no more, but we are here, aren't we? We will take his place. No one should cry any more.'

Pooling their money, they bought a huge rose garland and placed it on the body. When the bier set out, the three men shared the burden of carrying Appa, taking turns. His relatives and neighbours were truly amazed. They started speaking of Appa with pride.

Sangilimuthu sir said: 'Around two months before he died, your father was unable to walk any more. He struggled even to speak a few words. Seeing his plight, I told sir that he should quietly take leave from the school and look after his health. I told him as strongly as I was able to, but he wouldn't listen. He told me he would come to school even if he had to crawl. It was only after then that we made him sit on the bicycle and brought him to school every day.'

Dorairaj sir said: 'Was he ever afraid of his ailment? Not at all. Just sign your name, sit down and relax, sir, we told him. He wouldn't listen. Keeping some hot water on the table, which he would sip now and then, he carried on teaching the children something or the other.'

As the memories accumulated, the sorrow in his heart kept growing. Why had his father punished himself so, neither taking leave nor getting proper medical attention? Walking silently made him uncomfortable.

It was not polite of him to say nothing to the people who walked along with him, talking about his father. Since he didn't know what to say, he walked on, in spite of feeling awkward, till they finally reached Subramaniam sir's house.

Even before they arrived at the entrance of Subramaniam sir's house, his wife rushed out of the house and stood facing them. She looked at him with indescribable affection and anguish. Kamalathammal, the postman's wife, Pechchi paati and Coimbatore athai emerged from neighbouring houses and surrounded him.

Each woman showered him with her special affection. For him, their love was unbearably overt and formal. As though they had discussed and agreed on it beforehand, all the women treated him in the same way.

Taking more liberty than everyone else, Coimbatore athai embraced him and started crying while she kept babbling all manner of things. He was embarrassed even more. Distraught, he thought of possible ways to escape from the situation.

He started telling everyone about what Appa had said during his final days in the hospital, what he ate and how he died. Just when he ended his narration, two more people joined them. He recounted the same details to them. A few others arrived later. Every time new people dropped in, he had to repeat the same thing once again.

He narrated the same details over and over again, weaving his story with more or less the same words. Since they were details he had repeated to many people, he narrated them to everyone in the same way. Neither his words nor expressions changed even a whit. It was as though he was reciting from a written text.

In the end, he grew tired of it and felt irritated. His heart became wistful. His face broke out in a sweat. He trembled slightly.

Then Subramaniam sir said: 'All right. Leave him be. Let him eat. Ever since he arrived, we've kept him talking on no more than a cup of coffee. I wonder what he ate last, and at what time. Come, thambi, wash your hands. Let's eat.'

Dorairaj sir and Sangilimuthu sir, too, invited him to eat at their homes. He did not decline anybody's offer or invitation. He spoke to everyone tactfully and calmly. He spoke with caution, fearing his words might hurt someone. Inwardly, he was pleased at their display of affection, and prayed that no one would ever change their facial expressions of that moment.

Subramaniam sir's wife said: 'Sir was also like you, a guileless man. If he wanted something to eat, he would ask directly, without feeling shy. If he came in tired, he'd say, give me a tumbler of coffee, teacher-amma. Don't keep calling me teacher, sir. I don't even know how to sign my own name, I would tell him. What's the problem, teacher? A teacher's wife can only be a teacher, right? he'd say, and laugh heartily. Poor man, he was so pragmatic.'

A smile appeared on her lips as she stood there, sighing.

Subramaniam sir said as he ate: 'Pragmatic he certainly was, but he wasn't like that with everybody, was he? After that grocery store owner said what felt like a barb to him, sir did not speak to the fellow, looking properly at his face, till the very end. I was the one who told him: don't trouble yourself so much with cooking and stuff when you are ill; if you need something, ask me. Ask us if you want something to eat, don't feel shy. This is like your own home, I told him. He too felt and acted the same way.'

After lunch, everyone sat on rope cots laid out under the shade of a neem tree.

'We realized that the end was near. When sir was put on the bus and sent to your town, all of us went to the bus stop to see him off. Sangilimuthu sir went with him. We looked at sir's face at that time. We didn't know what was going on in his mind, but he kept staring at us. We were very worried. I wondered whether we were going to see him alive again. My eyes welled up with tears. Because I didn't want sir to see this, I wiped my tears with a towel while pretending to wipe my face.'

Even now, Dorairaj sir's eyes seemed to be shining with tears. He wiped his eyes with the end of his veshti and calmed down. Then Sangilimuthu sir, the postman's wife Kamalathammal, and Coimbatore athai started narrating their own memories of the departed man. They recounted a lot of things about Appa.

Then they sat around him. With paper and pen in hand, Dorairaj sir started writing. They toted up all the sums: the ten thousand rupees receivable on Appa's demise, his provident fund amount, gratuity and insurance amounts. They also added up the monies that Appa had borrowed from sundry people in the village and from his fellow teachers. Sangilimuthu sir had all the details noted in his diary.

Finally, Sangilimuthu, the eldest among them, spoke up: 'Thambi, as soon as you receive your father's dues, you must first settle all his debts. Spend the money prudently and responsibly. Get both your younger sisters married first. Then take good care of your mother. Your father loved her like his own life. You too must try to find a girl and get married. Isn't it your duty to live as a householder and prove yourself worthy of your father's name?'

They all left to look at the house where Appa had lived. The house rented by Appa was very small. Locked up for over four months, it was covered with dust and cobwebs. The air inside was musty and reeked of stale sweat.

Just as Subramaniam sir had told them, there weren't too many things in that house – just a couple of veshtis (an old and worn four-yard veshti with rents mended in many places; another two-yard veshti which was new and laundered), two shirts, undergarments and a towel. Besides these, a few aluminium utensils, a cooking stove, a tin trunk, a mat, a pillow and a blanket were all that they found in Appa's room.

Inside the trunk, they found Appa's degree certificate, an almanac, the diary gifted to Appa by his Karungalpalayam son-in-law, and a few letters addressed to him. There were many empty pages in the diary. Appa didn't get the chance to write in his diary this year. He had preserved the letters over many, many years. There was an old photo of Appa and Amma together and there was another one, taken many years ago, of Appa with his father. He felt happy to see his father as a handsome young man. Subramaniam sir told him that his father in that photograph looked like him and his grandfather resembled his father.

Appa's cycle had no air in its wheels. He gave away the cycle to the landlord in lieu of the rent owed by his father and packed the rest of the household objects in a bundle. The veshti and shirts smelled of Appa's sweat. Everyone had a distinct body smell, it seemed. Appa's distinct odour would linger in his clothes. He must not get these clothes washed so as to preserve that smell. The vessels had been touched by Appa's saliva. The letters addressed to him would reveal a lot about his life.

Except for Subramaniam sir, the rest took their leave and went away to mind their chores. Subramaniam sir alone came up to the bus stop. He was very angry with the other teachers.

'Look at them, thambi. They've left you alone. If something happens to them tomorrow, would you feel like staying with them till the end? They merely talk as if they have sugar on their tongue.'

'Why should we mind, sir? It doesn't matter.'

Even after he consoled Subramaniam sir, the man continued disparaging his fellow teachers until it was time for his bus to arrive. But the bus came into the stand only after a long delay. Subramaniam sir waited without getting irritated until then.

If Subramaniam sir hadn't come along, he would have had a hard time boarding the bus with his large bundle.

Later, when he recounted everything to his mother, she told him something in passing. It seemed that during Appa's last days, Subramaniam sir had quarrelled with him. As a result, he and Appa had not been on speaking terms for a long time.

Translated from the Tamil short story *Meethi* (1984).

A Person Named Das

Until two years ago, a person called Das with the identification marks as reported by Manju was living at the address indicated by her. Then suddenly he disappeared one day. The Malayali who lived now in the small house that Das had once rented knew nothing about him. Only the elderly woman from the neighbouring house still had a few memories of Das. She had immense regard and love for him. Owing to certain good traits he possessed, the person called Das had won the admiration of all the residents on that street. Das – who had no particular job and called himself a painter – painted billboards from time to time to earn a living. After his disappearance, several incomplete paintings were discovered in his small room. He was a solitary man; no one remembered any friend or relative coming to see him. It's not clear what happened in the interim, but a couple of years ago, he suddenly gave up painting billboards and stayed holed up in his room for as long as three months. Then, during the summer of that year, that is, in the second month after Manju and I got married, he disappeared. A month later, the lock on the door of his rented house was forced open. That apart, nothing more about him or his whereabouts was known. Das was an enigma for that old woman, the residents on that street, and for me too. He was not just an enigma for me; he was a sword hanging above my head, a noose around my neck.

The existence of this person called Das had landed me in a life-or-death situation.

'What was Das to you?' asked the old woman.

'Friend,' I said and walked out.

I walked down the road, stepping on the dark shadows of white gulmohur trees in full bloom. Dried up white gulmohur flowers were being trampled under my feet. The smoke-stained windows of neighbouring houses opened soundlessly. When I looked up, sensing eyes on my back, they closed in panic. Anxious faces behind those nervous window bars. Not just anxious, also fearful. The man had sown fear and anxiety before leaving. A seed germinates and grows into a plant. Its flowers become fruit, which ripen and drop to the ground. With every fruit that drops, plants sprout tenfold to turn the place into a jungle: a forest of anxiety. I knew that after I left, feet impelled by fear and disquiet would rush towards that house; the elderly lady who spoke to me would be bombarded with questions.

Where are you, Das? I want to see you. Why? Even God wouldn't know why. Das, you are not my friend; you are my enemy, a rival. You have already bested me in a race. Das, I am ready to concede my defeat at our very first meeting. Das, I will shake your hand and leave without a word, never looking back. I don't need anything else. I am no longer haunted by dreams.

Das, do you know what my dreams are like? No, you will never understand them; you don't need to, either. Das, I certainly won't tell you about them when we meet. But you have singed the wings of my dream, Das. It is lying on its back right now, writhing, thrashing its legs, on the verge of death. Do you hear its terminal wail, Das? I will show you my scorched left hand, Das. While talking to your elderly woman friend, I had shoved my left hand into my trouser pocket. If I had, due to a momentary lapse of attention, brought it out, she would have shouted in alarm. Das, I have never wanted to look at my amputated hand myself, with its bones sticking out. It terrifies me. I don't want to think about that moment again.

What kind of moment was it?

When I first heard of you two years ago, I laughed. After he told me about you in a hushed whisper, like a secret warning, my friend was shocked to see me laugh. Arrogance or excessive self-confidence, take your pick. Who is Das? Ha ha ha… just an ordinary person who paints billboards for a living, right? What a joke! Ha ha ha, with my education, my job, my wealth, my status, my personality… fool, don't utter the name Das ever again in my presence.

My laughter was loud enough to rattle the world. I banged on the table as though I was challenging someone. Das, if you were living on the same street then, you would have certainly heard the sound of my laughter. My friends, then at the height of their revelry, were scared; they turned pale and lifeless like corpses. After that day, no one has, on any occasion, taken your name within my earshot, Das. But at our engagement ceremony, when Manju was serving us coffee, I became nervous. You can't even imagine the evident contempt and rancour on her face then, Das. When she bent down to touch my feet, I quickly drew them back. However, on our wedding night, when she accepted my first kiss without resisting, when her arms embraced me as if from an involuntary reflex, it was then that I began to imagine that I had defeated you, Das.

Then, too, I wanted to laugh out loud.

But that was the moment when my blood vessels started to throb like violin strings. In the rapture induced by that first kiss, I lost track of you. When we had embraced, copulated, reached climax and experienced ecstasy with eyes closed, I heard a whisper in my ears like a rhythmic chant: 'Das, Das, Das.'

The aroma of flowers and the odour of sweat mingled in the breeze and made me feel dizzy. I couldn't open my eyes. The whispered chant, 'Das, Das, Das,' reached a crescendo, punching a hole in my eardrums. Its strings broken, my violin curled upon itself. Was I dreaming, then? Like a wraith, Manju sat kneeling in front of me. From her pale lips moving at an incredible speed issued an endless moan: 'Das, Das, Das.' Her face lined by beads of sweat was arranged like a chess game of grief. Her long hair hung loose over her voluptuous breasts streaked with fingernail marks. Her hair swayed in the wind like a figure-hugging black garment she was born with. She had covered her navel with both hands. Her body was shaking and rocking in a kind of dance movement: a reckless, fiendish whirl. In some remote corner of my mind's expanse, I heard the insistent thrumming of a hand-drum.

Das, my blood stream dried up instantly. I was still as a corpse for a brief while. Then my blood vessels swelled. My body grew hot and blood rushed to my head. I leapt up and grabbed her hair. Yelling 'stop, stop!' or something equivalent, I shook her wildly. Manju slid away effortlessly from my hands like a snake. As if she was pleading for refuge, she started yelling and shouting, 'Das, Das, Das!' My anger peaked. Completely losing control of myself, I began to assault her. Holding her hair in a bunch, I slapped her again and again on the face and back, and pushed her on the floor. She didn't yield even then; she leapt up in a second. As if in retaliation, she yelled 'Das, Das, Das,' even more intensely than before.

I have no idea how long this went on, but I grew tired. Exhausted, I collapsed face down on the bed. She was sobbing. Her body had blood-red welts all over. Blood streaked out of both corners of her mouth, spattering on the bed and all over the room. Even when she was beaten and lying on the floor, her posture did not change. Her body was swaying like a dancer's. And through her body's tremors, she mumbled: 'Das, Das, Das.'

Das, most likely it was at that moment that I began to sense defeat for the first time. At the same time, I wondered if there was any way I could make her aware of herself and stop what she was doing. I don't know what I was feeling at that moment, but suddenly I began to cry. Though I didn't even have the slightest urge to cry, a sob rose involuntarily from the pit of my stomach. Completely losing self-control, I began to scream and wail. Manju's voice also rose to rival mine. 'Das, Das, Das.' Her yell was louder than mine. Not wanting to concede defeat, I began to wail even louder. My wails, her screams and the echo produced by their bouncing off the walls of that room combined to render the atmosphere grotesque. Neither she nor I was going to yield. One of us had to face defeat.

Das, it had turned into a challenge. It was either you or me. However, Das, I was defeated this time too. I couldn't wail continuously. My voice broke and became raspy. Blood flowed out of my mouth and drenched my chest. Finally, Das, only air came out of my throat. But Manju was screaming louder than ever before. 'Das, Das, Das…' God, don't forsake me. Das, I sought refuge in my god. I don't want anything else. Just give me the strength to sob and weep, I said. But, Das, my god had abandoned me.

That horrible moment occurred then, Das. Like everything else, this too happened involuntarily. I did only what any man forsaken by god would do in that situation. Das, my world turned dark. Lying face down on the bed, I felt that those were my final moments. My breath was ebbing away. But what kind of death was in the offing for me? 'Das, Das, Das.' All around me, the sound of my rival's name was being intoned like a chant, and I was forced to hear it… God, I could not allow it. Somehow, before the thread of my breathing snapped, I had to stop this. It was then that it happened. Das, I had perhaps turned insane. Listen to this.

On the shelf at the head of our nuptial bed, I found a brand new candle and a box of matches. I didn't know why they had been kept there. They were perhaps meant to be used by the newlyweds in the event of an emergency, like a power shutdown. But I hadn't noticed them until that moment. Now I chanced upon them at first glance. That was the reason for all that followed later. If I had looked at some other object, things might have turned out differently. Das, without any plan in my mind, I crawled towards that candlestick. Not knowing why, I lit the candle and placed it before me. For a short while, I gazed at the flame which was burning slowly and steadily. More ferocious now than ever before, Manju slapped the floor repeatedly with both hands, shouting 'Das, Das, Das' maliciously and dancing frenetically like an ogre. Her hair spun around in a whirl. Her shadow cast by the candle flame grew gigantic and its dancing shape folded itself along the wall, floor and ceiling. I sat immobile, staring in silence at the burning candle flame, Manju and her shadow, and listening to her screams: 'Das, Das, Das.' I don't how much time passed in this way. In the end, I don't know why I did it, but I broke into a smile. In my mind's eye, I saw my own face. Das, I had never seen my face so clear and peaceful before.

Then I held my left index finger, slowly and deliberately, over the candle flame, which was burning bright. In that instant, the flame trembled and leaned away, wavered slightly and then hesitantly kissed my finger. The heat entered my blood stream with a sting, like venom. Then my whole finger caught fire and began to burn. The flesh of my finger burned and crackled, with fat rising to the surface. At the same time, a sob rose from my stomach. The next moment, it came out as a loud scream. The room itself trembled and shook. Cracks appeared on the walls. Das, you will never know the ecstasy that overtook me in that moment. Screaming, I offered one more finger to the burning flame. The fire drew my finger in and began to feast on it greedily. Then I offered another. The fire spread fast and began to scorch my whole left hand. Manju had stopped her screaming long ago. When I saw her looking stunned, not knowing what to do, frozen like a corpse with its eyes open, I burst out laughing. I had begun to laugh spitefully, explosively, loud enough to shake the world. While I was still laughing, I lost consciousness.

Das, what happened next is not important. It was in that moment that I developed a strong urge to meet you. I began to look for you everywhere. But you were in too much of a hurry. You ran away too soon. You are an idiot, Das. Crazy fool, you don't get it, do you? Das, where are you? I need to see you, Das.

Translated from the Tamil short story *Das Enbavanum Das Enbavanum* (1996).

The Tool of His Trade

Thangarasu tailor sold off his old sewing machine. There was no other way out for him.

Was it a machine at all when he sold it?

To have kept it for so long was no mean achievement. He had endured all its torments only because he wanted to hold on to this last remnant of the dowry from his wife's parents. It wasn't his lawful wedded wife, after all, that he had to put up with it forever.

Thangarasu had always got a special kick out of comparing the machine with his wife Soundhiram. His love for the machine was not a whit less than the affection he showered on her.

In the past, he had quarrelled with his wife and packed her off to her parents' house. He had even thought about getting rid of her, once for all. But Thangarasu tailor could never contemplate parting with, leave alone getting rid of, his machine.

As a child is to the mother and a field ox to the farmer, so the sewing machine was to Thangarasu tailor.

When he sat in front of the machine and started sewing, his whole demeanour was transformed. By nature, Thangarasu was a rough sort. But as soon as he sat at his machine, that roughness disappeared somewhere; instead, he was overcome with shyness and exultation, as if touching a new bride. When he got four or five orders together for new dresses, he even offered a special puja to the machine.

As soon as he opened his shop in the morning, he polished the machine to shine like a mirror; nothing less would please him. He oiled it frequently. On Fridays, after adorning it with a string of flowers, he waved a camphor flame in front of the sewing machine and lit incense sticks. He was very vigilant about not allowing anyone apart from himself to come anywhere close to it.

He would often scold the machine as though it were animate and had feelings, or whack it hard with a pair of scissors. During moments of great stress, he was even ready to give up his profession. But his love for the machine did not waver at any time.

But all this was a long time ago, perhaps ten or fifteen years back.

The day he brought Soundhiram as a new bride to Loganathapuram was the happiest ever in Thangarasu tailor's life. The entire population of that locality was amazed and delighted at Soundhiram's arrival. The houses of Loganathapuram hung with tattered jute curtains and its streets pervaded by gutter stench and rotting garbage welcomed her with boundless love. To have such a beauteous girl coming to live in Loganathapuram was an honour far exceeding what those streets and houses deserved. Not all girls in Loganathapuram were unsightly, though.

Unni Mary, Keshavan Nair's wife, had an uneven row of teeth but her eyes were beautiful, like a mullet's. Though Vasantha Ruby, Thomas mechanic's eldest daughter, sported a largish nose, which other girl could match her long, thick, jet-black hair? Subramaniam Gounder's wife Sampooranam was dark, yes, but women with her voluptuous figure were rare. The beauty of Parimala's eyebrows, Elizabeth teacher's rows of pearly white teeth, Usha Rani's rosy feet and calves streaked with down – you could look at them for as many hours as you wanted without feeling tired.

Though all this was true, everyone readily agreed that Soundhiram possessed, in her single person, all the aforesaid markers of physical beauty.

However, apart from Soundhiram, there was another reason for Thangarasu tailor's delight and pride. The arrival at his doorstep by horse cart of a brand new sewing machine, a dowry from his father-in-law, had made him doubly happy.

To everyone who dropped by to look at his new bride, he showed off his machine and sought their opinion. While prostrating at the feet of elders for their blessings, he boasted: 'See the machine I've got? Doesn't it look just like Karna Maharaja's chariot?'

For him, it was a matter of deep regret that he couldn't bring the machine along when he took his wife to the tent theatre, bazaar or on visits to relatives' houses.

On the third day after its arrival, Thangarasu rented a shop beside the big portia tree in Loganathapuram and set up his new machine. He named his shop 'Soundhiram Tailors' and started plying his trade. Soundhiram performed several rounds of *dhrishti* for both the machine and Thangarasu to ward off evil eyes.

The shop did very well during the initial months. Thangarasu lived happily, looking after his wife with as much love and care as he lavished on the machine. But there is such a thing called time, isn't there? Does it ever stand still?

Take an example: our country, which is a free nation now, was still a slave to the white man when Thangarasu was born. Thangarasu was not a tailor then either, nor was tailoring his career of choice at the time. As a child, when his father yelled at him, 'Go to school, da!' he went. Later one day, his father said, 'You've had enough schooling. Go apprentice yourself in a tailoring shop,' and placed him with Sayabu tailor. Obeying his father's command, Thangarasu started training to work as a tailor.

At first he stitched buttonholes by hand; later, he sewed buttons.

Initially, he hadn't liked his vocation at all. Sayabu, coughing incessantly from bronchitis, had adopted cuffing Thangarasu frequently on the head and pinching him sharply on the thigh as duties appropriate for a master.

The little boy Thangarasu, fearful of his guru's aforesaid proclivities, kept sewing buttons with his head bowed, never looking up. 'When you're free, go over to the machine and practise tailoring,' his father urged him. But whenever he went near the machine, Sayabu hit him with a pair of tailoring scissors.

Poor Thangarasu.

He believed firmly that he was never going to learn tailoring from that Sayabu; that he would keep stitching buttonholes and sewing buttons all his living days; that as long as he possessed a head and had flesh on his thighs, this Sayabu would cuff him on the head and pinch him on the thighs.

Countless summers, winters and the seasons of rain and wind arrived in their turn, year after year. Even the games children played – gilli, top, kabaddi and marbles – changed frequently. These changes came about without any particular effort from anyone. However, no matter how much he tried, Thangarasu could not to go beyond stitching buttonholes, sewing buttons and suffering corporal punishment from Sayabu.

'Whatever happens, I won't go to Sayabu tailor's any more,' he declared one day. But on that day, instead of Sayabu tailor, it was his father who scolded and thrashed him. He preferred getting this treatment from Sayabu tailor; Sayabu at least bought him a cup of tea when it was nearing dusk.

So, resolved that this was his fate and it would never change, Thangarasu continued to perform his daily chores.

However, contrary to what Thangarasu had imagined, he did learn tailoring well. Once he attained the status of an independent tailor, he married Soundhriam, received a brand new sewing machine as dowry, and set up a tailoring shop in Loganathapuram. How life had changed for him!

That the country, which was a colony under the white man when Thangarasu was born, became independent later has already been mentioned. But Thangarasu was not aware of the change for a long time. But no one could blame him for that lapse.

When the country gained freedom at midnight, Thangarasu was fast asleep. He was a little boy then. Since he did not know that the country was going to become independent later that night, he came home from the shop, ate his gruel and went to sleep. As soon as he fell asleep, Sayabu appeared in his dreams. Even in the dream, Sayabu was his usual self: he cuffed and pinched Thangarasu. At the very first cuff, Thangarasu's skull was broken and blood gushed out. The flesh on his thigh was yanked out till only the bone was left. Sayabu twisted Thangarasu's ears and then the head itself disappeared. Sayabu had looked normal at first, seated at his sewing machine and coughing incessantly. The next moment he was sitting on a buffalo's back. Both his eyes were large as coconuts. His whole beard was bunched into a big moustache on his face and his measuring tape had morphed into his lasso of death. Sayabu came in hot pursuit of Thangarasu, roaring now instead of coughing relentlessly…

'Buttonhole, button, Lord of Death, his lasso, measuring tape, skull, thigh, blood, aiyo…' Poor Thangarasu woke up screaming. Alarmed and concerned that something had happened to their son, his father and mother calmed him down and made him go back to sleep. Amid all the commotion, Thangarasu did not learn about India becoming independent that night. Even now, he didn't know much about any of that. His life was confined to his home and his work. When he grew up and became eligible to vote, and somebody called him to vote, Thangarasu asked him,

'Vote-aa? What is that? Why should I vote?'

'We have to choose our own leaders, Thangarasu... Ours is a free country, don't you know that?'

This was the sum of what Thangarasu knew about the nation's independence.

Even if many such changes took place without Thangarasu tailor being aware of them, he had not really gained or lost a great deal in consequence. However, only when the number of families and residents in Loganathapuram increased and still newer tailoring shops had sprouted here and there was Thangarasu able to understand that events in the outside world could also affect his life.

First, Bahadur tailor's shop came up in Kattabomman street.

Young Bahadur knew how to stitch clothes in the modern style. The man too looked handsome and stylish. He sat in his shop dressed in a different outfit every day, always looking tip-top. His manner suggested that he was testimony to his own professional skill. Even the name he had chosen for his shop was very appealing. It was the name of a voluptuous actress who was then at the peak of her popularity. In ninety-nine per cent of her films, she danced semi-naked, dressed only in her undergarments. As soon as Bahadur named his shop after an actress who never wore any clothes and hung up her portrait, the citizens of Loganathapuram started frequenting his shop, if only to pass the time.

Such ploys were beyond Thangarasu's capacity. First, no matter how hard he tried, Thangarasu could not turn into a young man like Bahadur tailor. Second, he was no expert in stitching clothes in the modern style like Bahadur was. At his age, he couldn't really apprentice himself to a tailor, enduring cuffs on the head and verbal abuses, just to learn the modern style, could he? Nor could he afford to employ such a tailor in his shop.

Feeding four people and sending his two children to school were onerous tasks in themselves. There were two reasons why Thangarasu tailor sent his children to school. First, he did not want his two children to grow up ignorant like him. Though he himself didn't know when the country had gained independence, at least his children should grow up knowing something about current events. Such was his wish. Second, he didn't want his children to become tailors like him, hard put to earn even their daily bread; he wanted them to study well and take up white-collar jobs.

Moreover, Thangarasu tailor's machine was not as new as Bahadur tailor's. It had become old, and several parts had become damaged. Because of the loud clatter that rose whenever he sat down at his machine to work, neighbouring citizens of Loganathapuram had begun to think of him as their mortal enemy. Hanging up the picture of a screen vamp was the only thing he could do in that situation. As for the shop's name, he was of the firm opinion that no other name could be more appealing than Soundhiram.

It slowly became clear to Thangarasu tailor that he simply could not compete professionally with Bahadur.

So what?

Would the planter fail to water the sapling? Would their Creator forget to feed them regularly? What was he going to achieve by scrambling to earn a lot of money? Four small stomachs in his family – how could they go empty? Come what may, his family would live as they did now. Thangarasu began to console himself by indulging in such philosophical reflections.

However, the march of time did not spare him. Just as Bahadur had set up shop in Kattabomman street, Peter and Raghavan settled down with their sewing machines in Anna and Ambedkar streets respectively. But neither their professional skill nor the appeal of their shops put any fresh dent in Thangarasu tailor's fortunes. By then his sewing machine had already become unfit for sewing. One or two orders for dresses turned up once in a rare while. But Thangarasu had neither the thread for sewing nor oil for lubricating his machine. If he completed the job by borrowing some money from the customer himself, he was left with a rupee or two for his labours.

Even that piffling amount had to be smuggled home to Soundhiram after proffering clever excuses and abject pleas to a phalanx of dunning creditors. Only then would she feed him gruel without showering him with abuses. Or else…

'You call yourself a man! Do you see other men carrying on like you? If a family man won't even earn a tumbler of rice in a day, how can the woman run the household? Those two children – if they don't go to the workshop at their age and earn a couple of rupees, there will be no food. You said you will educate them, you couldn't even do that!'

Thangarasu's only answer to her was silence. Poor thing, what could she do? She was just like the machine she had brought with her as dowry. Like so many women, she too stepped into her husband's home laden with many dreams about the future. But life brought her only grief and tears.

Even in the face of such penury, Thangarasu held on to his machine. Instead of sitting in his shop and waiting for the orders, he started going where the orders were. He fitted a wooden plank with caster wheels, placed his machine on it and wheeled it all over the locality, mending old clothes.

Did it matter where he plied his trade? He did not steal, lie or cheat anyone, did he? He tried to cope with life's challenges by working honestly to earn his daily bread.

However, since the protagonist of our story is neither a political leader nor a character in a movie, throwing and accepting challenges were matters he was not used to.

Could a man ever challenge his creditor?

Thangarasu tailor was forced to sell his machine because he could no longer fend off his creditors. We don't have to go into the antecedents of how Thangarasu got himself into debt.

All that was quite normal.

We hear that there are innumerable crorepatis in our country like the Tatas and Birlas. Even they are reported to be in debt to the tune of hundreds of crores. India is such a big country; even so, it owes thousands of crores to America.

Compared to our great nation, what was Thangarasu?

Just an ordinary tailor. He too owed someone two hundred and fifty rupees. On that fateful day when his creditor tracked down Thangarasu with his machine and held him captive with a towel around his shoulders, Thangarasu had no other option.

He sold his machine.

He had scolded that machine so often, kicked it a few times. He had even looked forward to the day when he would be rid of it. But the way he brooded and cried inwardly when it left him was a secret no one else came to know.

What would Thangarasu do now? It was something he himself didn't know.

After paying off his creditor, Thangarasu took the few remaining rupees and went to a liquor shop. It was a long time since the machine had earned him so much money. With bloodshot eyes, he staggered from the liquor shop all the way to Loganathapuram.

Bahadur Tailors on Kattabomman street was humming with activity. Thangarasu stood and stared at the shop. New machine. Bahadur tailor, still a young man. Seeing him, Thangarasu tailor recalled the times when he had sat at his machine as a young man. His eyes filled with tears.

Reeling on unsteady feet, he entered the shop. He grabbed the remaining notes from his inner pocket and held them bunched up in his fist.

'Bahadur!'

He held the rupee notes directly in front of Bahadur's face, spreading them in display.

'See, I've sold the machine. Do you know how long I had had that machine with me? I nurtured it like my own child. I sold it today. What kind of machine was it? Only fit for plucking pubic hair. With that machine, you couldn't even mend old clothes. To hell with it! Never mind, I'll get another one. A new machine, I'll show you! I'll buy a machine newer than yours! Do you think I am babbling after a few drinks? Yes, I've had a few. I drank for fifteen rupees, do you know that? What's the big deal? I'll drink even more. I'll drink for all the money in my pocket. What do I need money for, it's like pubic hair to me. Do you feel like a drink?'

Thangarasu quarrelled with Bahadur tailor. The story of how he bought the machine, sold it, its great features – he narrated everything over and over again, and then wept. He will narrate the same story to many more people.

He will tell it to Peter tailor on Anna street, Raghavan tailor on

Ambedkar street, and to all other residents of Loganathapuram. He will narrate it whenever he comes across a human face.

He will talk about his machine to his wife Soundhiram and his children too; he will end up weeping. He will also quarrel with them.

My pen is not potent enough to describe all that he might do.

Translated from the Tamil short story *Karuvi* (1983).

The Curse of Resurrection

With the pot of holy water on his shoulder, Nallaan hurried, panting, along a jungle trail flanked by dense thickets and strewn with rosary peas. As he walked, he kept chanting the obscure phrases taught to him by the hermit. Fortunately, it hadn't rained that day. Otherwise, the flood of rainwater would have washed the peas away and he would have lost his way. His younger sister Nallaal, who was in the forest with her seven children, had scattered those rosary peas all along her trail.

It was a childhood game for the two siblings.

The forest was full of countless jamun trees and butterflies. Both siblings used to roam the dense parts of this jungle all through the day, plucking jamuns and chasing butterflies. Nallaal would often venture alone into the jungle. On each outing, she scattered rosary peas with their black heads and red bodies all along her path, one at every step. Using them as traces, Nallaan could always find her, no matter which corner of the jungle she was in. Picking up and gathering the scattered rosary peas in a pouch at his waist, he followed the path along which the scatter of peas led. Where the trail of rosary peas ended, Nallaal appeared with a smile as purple as the inside of a jamun fruit. Else, she was crouched inside a bush, watching the frolic of birds. Or she was gathering and stitching nettles together inside a bush of cow's thorn to trap butterflies. Sometimes

Nallaan became angry, perhaps fatigued from wandering all over the jungle looking for her. As soon as he spotted Nallaal, he approached her furtively from behind and laid a lash on her back with a supple twig. Ripe jamun fruit and rosary peas spilled out from a fleeing Nallaal's lap. Butterflies flitted past them, displaying all the colours of a rainbow.

Nallaal would come home and sulk for a long time. Then Nallaan returned the jamun fruit and rosary peas that she had spilled and left behind. He would have picked them again in the forest and saved them in his waist pouch before returning home. Her tears vanished as soon as she saw them. 'My sweet brother,' she would fling her arms around his neck in a hug. Collecting her rosary peas in a mud bowl, she kept it safely in a secret hiding place; she also changed this hiding place often. After she got married and left to live with her in-laws, Nallaan discovered one such mud bowl at home. Later, he put away the mud bowl and the rosary peas in it safely, keeping them as mementos of his sister.

Nallaan heard the story from his workers when he returned from his journey: that after many years Nallaal had come to her native home with her seven children; that Alankari had refused to let her in and bolted the door from inside; that Alankari had abused her with vile words and chased her away along with her seven children; that, expecting her brother to return soon, Nallaal had spent the night in the cattle shed, huddled under a blanket with her children, enduring the endless annoyance of mosquitoes; that she had left the village at dawn, distraught and in tears, and entered the forest as a helpless, abandoned woman. A broken pot made of unfired clay and the charred remains of a green plantain stem that she had used to light a makeshift stove lay at the entrance. A few crows were busy feeding on the tiny morsels of half-cooked rice which lay scattered inside.

Nallaan first looked for the bowl containing his sister's rosary peas. The bowl was lying upside down on the floor, with a few peas scattered around it. Only then did Nallaan proceed to the foot trail that led into the forest. He walked in solitude, with only his childhood memories for company, down the path marked by the rosary peas. At the spot where the trail ended, there was an abandoned well. Nallaan saw the well, its dilapidated parapet made of stone, and eight pairs of nervous footprints crisscrossing the ground around the parapet. Stomach shuddering in fear, he peeped in. The gold pendant of his sister Nallaal's thali glittered on the clear bed of sand at the bottom of the well. Even the ripples hadn't died down yet. He felt a small hope rise in his heart. It was unlikely that a lot of time had elapsed. Without a second thought, he dived into the well. Using his strong shoulders, he dragged all eight bodies out of the well, one by one, and laid them on the ground. The bodies still had a little warmth left. Nallaan rubbed the soles of their feet to make them warm, pressed on their chests to eject the water they had swallowed and blowed into their mouths to resuscitate their breathing, but to no avail. With mounting grief, he sat slumped against the well's ruined parapet and sobbed his heart out.

Later, his tears spent, he tried to lay the scattered bodies face up and arrange them in a row. As he turned over his sister Nallaal's corpse, he noticed her arms, which were swollen from banging repeatedly on the bolted door of his house. 'Nalla, my darling!' His wail carried in all directions and shook the whole world. It was then that Nallaan remembered the hermit. He had a long-standing association with the hermit who constantly roamed the forests, eager to learn the secrets of life and death. Nallaan felt that if he met the hermit and spoke to him, he would find a reprieve from this terrible tragedy.

After covering all the eight bodies with pine leaves, he set out in search of the hermit. He wandered along the trails inside the forest, scattering rosary peas. After two moonlit nights and a whole day, he located the object of his quest. The hermit looked very old, with his head of grey hair and shrunken body. He was sitting cross-legged in a rock cleft. Without putting any question to Nallaan who came and knelt in front of him with tears in his eyes, the hermit quickly whispered the life-giving mantra in Nallaan's ears. Then the hermit gave him a pot filled with holy water and bade him to return immediately. Nallaan started his return journey without even thinking of paying his respects to the hermit and taking his leave properly. He walked at a faster pace than before. His body bore wounds all over from being scratched by thorns. He was gnawed by worry that the bodies might have decomposed. It was noon by the time he reached the well. A mild stench had begun to spread in the air around the bodies. A black beetle emerged with great difficulty from his sister Nallaal's nostril, fluttered its wings and flew away.

Was it the bird of life, perhaps?

He sprinkled holy water on all the bodies. Then he walked ritually around them, constantly chanting the mantra given by the hermit. A long time passed, but there was no stir of life in them. The earth was rotating. It rotated at several times its usual speed, whirling around itself. In an instant, the day vanished into night. The night, too, lasted only a moment. The next moment happened to be the evening of the following day. Childhood memories churned violently in his mind. Drowned in memories that led him to the times he had roamed the forest with his sister, he forgot the hermit's mantra. Only later did he hear his sister's call:

'Anna!'

'Anna… Anna!'

When he opened his eyes, he saw Nallaal and her seven children standing around him. Nallaal beamed at him, her face radiant with the innocence and unrestrained joy of a child. 'Nalla, my darling! So, nothing terrible has happened to you and the children!' Eyes streaming with tears, he hugged them all.

'Wait, Anna! I'll be right back.' Nallaal slid away from his embrace and ran happily to the bank of a nearby stream. The children followed her, shouting with excitement. Trailing them, Nallaan too reached the bank. They all drank the clear water from the stream and quenched their thirst. There were many tiny butterflies flitting in and out of the thickets on the bank. 'Amma, catch some butterflies for us!' The children hugged their mother's legs.

Nallaal once again turned into a little girl who pulled out plants of cow's thorn and wove nettles into a trap for butterflies. Nallaan turned into a little boy who sat on a rock gazing at them.

The sister came to him with a bag full of butterflies. The children couldn't contain their joy. Each child grabbed a couple of butterflies. To help them play the game of tying butterflies together, Nallaal unravelled threads from the end of her sari and gave them to the children. The remaining butterflies swarmed over her body, mistaking her for a flower. They perched like a garland of flowers on her long tresses. They crawled and wandered across her nostrils and earlobes. Nallaal laughed bashfully. Nallaan was worried.

'We're getting late! Let's go, Nalla.'

'Where to, Anna?' asked Nallaal innocently.

'Home, Nalla. Where else?'

'Whose home, Anna?'

'What kind of a question is that? To our home, Nalla,' replied a confused Nallaan. He didn't understand the real meaning of his sister's question.

She remained silent. Her face grew dark, and a deep sigh escaped her. Then she said: 'Now, there is no home that can be identified as common to both of us, Anna.' As she finished saying those words, Nallaan noticed that her eyes had welled up. By then, all her seven children had come there.

Discreetly, without their noticing it, Nallaal wiped her tears and laughed: 'Done with playing for the day?'

'Amma, we are hungry,' cried the children.

'I'll pluck you jamun fruit.' She led them all to the ancient jamun tree next to the abandoned well. The children were very excited. One of them tried to climb the tree. 'Wait,' Nallathangaal stopped him; then she hitched her sari up between the knees and tied it firmly before clambering up the tree herself.

Nallaan stood up. 'Thanga, wait. I'll pluck them for you,' he ran to the tree. 'You might fall down.'

Nallaal laughed. By then, she had climbed up the tree and reached the high branches laden with fruit.

'This tree is mine, Anna. I've eaten its maiden crop.' Then she asked her children who were standing around the trunk: 'Do you all want roasted fruit… or ripe fruit? Tell me, my darlings!'

'We want roasted fruit!' they cried.

Nallaal pressed down on a branch and shook it hard. The fruit showered down on the ground. Jamun fruit with glistening black skin. Nallaan, too, turned into a child as he shouted: 'I want ripe fruit, Nalla!' After plucking and gathering a few red-coloured fruit with an astringent taste, Nallaal jumped down. Later, the two siblings sat on a rock with their legs stretched out and ate the jamun fruit.

'Do you remember our childhood, Anna?'

'I can never forget anything related to our childhood, Nalla!'

'Remember, we used to set out for the fields with our father at the crack of dawn?'

'Our father always walked ahead, leading the bulls. We followed him, tracing his footsteps. I remember it very well...' said Nallaan. He, too, was lost in childhood memories.

'He carried the hoe on his shoulder, Anna!'

'Amma walked behind, carrying the seed basket. There was food for all of us inside the basket. And our puppy came along with us too, reluctant to be parted from our company. Remember that puppy?'

'In the fields, we often fought with each other.'

'You had to compete with me for every little thing. You even wanted to hold the plough. Amma stopped you. That's not girls' work, she'd say. But you never listened. Right from ploughing the field to harvesting the grain, you wanted to contribute to everything. Your sweat is present in every bit of this earth, Nalla.'

'Both of us worked hard, Anna!'

'Your blood, too, has mixed with this earth, Nalla. You were injured here many times, weren't you?'

'It was your blood as well, Anna. You were wounded, too!'

'This is our land,' said Nallaan. His voice trembled.

'But that's not how it works, Anna. Now this land belongs only to you. That's what your wife told me last night. Now I've lost my right to even a single grain from this field, Anna. This is the house where I was born; a place where I crawled, learned to walk and grew up. It has seven doors. Not one of them opened for me and my children. I was forced to leave with my hungry children in search of this old, abandoned well, Anna.'

Nallaal wept with unbearable sorrow. Nallaan was distraught.

Tears filled his eyes too. His blood began to boil. 'I'll take revenge on her!' He stood up.

'Who, just who are you going to take revenge on, the wife you are united with in holy matrimony?'

'She is the one responsible for these calamities!'

'What wrong has she done, Anna?' asked Nallaal, laughing. 'For her, it's her home. She is a girl, after all. It's the way of the world, isn't it? A girl's native home is not permanent. I am the living proof of that. Don't turn her into the proof of how a girl's married home is also not permanent, Anna. Let her live on with her dreams.'

Ineffable clarity in her voice, along with an incredible resolve: was it the effect of resurrection?

'All right. Let's go, Nalla. We'll go home. If you come with me, my childhood will come back. It will be like a resurrection for me, Nalla. Come home. I'll catch some spotted deer and singing parrots for your children to play with.' Forgetting his grief, Nallaan returned to his childhood.

'You're trying to lure us, aren't you?' Nallaal laughed.

'What right do I have to come to your house? What statement would I make by returning there? When people ask, what answer will you or I give them? I won't be the only one to suffer humiliation. I might fall prey to an endless feeling of guilt, Anna! Please forgive me!'

Nallaan felt a lump in his throat.

'Are you asking me to leave you and your children alone in this jungle? How can I do that?'

The sister smiled.

'I am not without succour, Anna. I have seven children with me. And there will be no death for us any more. The secret of the mantra that the hermit taught you is known to me too. Once resurrected, you never die again. You knew this, and yet you brought us back to life. This is an eternal curse for us. Leave us to wander and roam with the burden of this curse, Anna.'

Then, along with her seven children, Nallathangaal disappeared into the dense darkness of the jungle. He pleaded and cried. Her heart was unmoved. Before she left, she received a boon from her brother that he would never tell the world about her and the children being resurrected.

'Those deaths must not be in vain. Let the world keep thinking about them, feel humiliated, and be racked by guilt. Let many questions arise from this life and death, Anna! Then there might be an end to these horrible tragedies. Call me then, and I'll come. Don't tell anyone, Anna!'

A boon or a curse?

Nallaan returned home with his head in a muddle. Just as she had asked him, he never confided anything to anyone. But just has he had vowed to do, he killed his wife, chopping her into little pieces. For Alankaari it was liberation. After hearing from the goatherds that Nallathangaal and her seven children had killed themselves by jumping into an abandoned well, she had been suffering from a terrible sense of guilt.

11

Later, her curse came true. There was no rain for several years. Lakes and ponds went dry. The land became a desert. Even that abandoned well dried up. The suffering of the people was unsightly. This famine was crueller than the one that had driven her along with her seven children from her in-laws' house to her native home. It was the result of her curse. As her anger subsided, she became merciful. She found a goatherd in the jungle and told him about her curse.

Then the village came awake and engaged briskly in deeds of atonement. They erected a temple for her in the outskirts of the village. They installed idols of her and the seven children, and worshipped them. The abandoned well was named after her. A poet narrated her story as a series of ballads. A barber who heard them went from village to village, singing her story as he plied his trade. Through listening to it till the wee hours of dawn and weeping relentlessly, the world got a reprieve from her curse. It started to rain. Within a few years, the soil had recovered its fertility. Then, every village in the world constructed a temple for her and an abandoned well next to it, and worshipped her.

For all chaste women, she became a guardian angel. An angel who gave them the boon of surviving famine, hunger, starvation and unbearable sorrow. Terrible famines were named after Nallathangaal. Affectionate brothers were called Nallaan and their wives were called Mooli Alankaari. Unaware of these developments, Nallathangaal roamed the forest with her children, free of all cares. Her children enjoyed playing with spotted deer and laughed merrily as they conversed with singing parrots.

III

Ages passed by.

Nallathangaal was soon fed up of the jungle. She craved human company again. For how many years could she keep talking to the parrots? Moreover, she wanted to see the state of the world after so many years. The world had developed in a different way in her imagination. She thought that her life now would seem implausible to anyone. First, she wanted to see the abandoned well and the temple erected for her by the village. She also wanted to visit her native home. Even after ages, kin was still kin, after all! One evening she left the forest with her seven children and emerged into the world. There was no grievance in her heart. She walked towards her native village as a totally free person, without any fear or anxiety.

She couldn't see the abandoned well. There was a hamlet where the well used to be. So what? She didn't need to see the traces of what was past. The village had changed completely. But for her gut instinct, she wouldn't even have recognized it as her own. But she did find a temple in an abandoned and unkempt piece of land on the outskirts of the village. The temple, too, was dilapidated. Inside the temple, beneath the cover of wild scrub she discovered clay figures depicting her and her seven children. Two of the children were headless. She stood at the centre, with her arms around the children. The sculptor had shaped each figure with great attention to detail, as if he had each person standing in front of him. Her figure was missing an arm. Her hair was untied and hanging loose. Her wide eyes were filled with the sorrow of helplessness. Three children were nestled in the embrace of her left arm. It was the right arm which held the remaining four that was missing. She wanted to find the missing arm. She and her children together retrieved it from the bushes. The children touched and caressed it with their fingers. One boy juxtaposed that fragment with the mother's real hand. It matched her hand perfectly, as though it had been cast in a mould. There was one minor flaw, however. The palm was bigger. It couldn't have been an inadvertent mistake. She wondered what could have caused it. Only then did she recall the time, ages ago, when she had knocked relentlessly on the door of her maternal home, pleading for it to be opened, and the resulting pain and swelling in her right palm. The swollen palm had healed later, but the sculptor had not forgotten. Could her brother have told the sculptor? Was she dwelling on the past again? No!

The village had turned upside down. Modern streets, lined with even more modern houses. But there was no change in the design of doors. Each door had a latch. It must have been a day of celebration. There was an intolerable crush of crowds on the streets. Everywhere, bodies adorned with new clothes. Faces exultant with joy. The rumble of revelry from all directions. The ecstasy of laughter. No shadow of grief clouded anyone's brow.

The old era had passed. It had been an era of terrible tragedies. The sorrow of mankind had drowned along with her in that abandoned well. She, with her seven children, had entered a new era, resplendent and free of the curse. A welcome move, certainly. The world didn't have to remember her any more; or Alankaari, who had shut her door on them and driven her to the abandoned well; or that well itself, a monument to grief. There was no longer any need for her dilapidated shrine or its maimed sculptures. It was all a tale, merely an ancient tale. Even that tale need not be narrated by anyone to his neighbour.

The carousels were spinning.

Children were riding on the revolving wooden horses. Their mothers who looked on felt the sway of elation in their bodies. Her seven children gazed at the carousel in wonder. It looked like they, too, wished to ride the carousel. They had known only the forests since the day there were born, after all. If her brother had been around, he would have put up a golden swing for them. The man in charge of the carousel told her, 'The children want to ride the carousel, it seems. Put them aboard, lady!' She hesitated. But her children accepted his invitation and climbed on the ride. The carousel spun. The giant canopy fixed on the top of its axle moved slowly. The children laughed. There was a slight trace of fear on the younger one's face. One of the older boys reassured him. He held the reins of the horse with a cavalryman's élan. He had learnt horse riding as a child, after all. When she was tossing the children, one by one, into the ruined well, he was the one who blocked her. 'I'll feed all of you, Amma. I can work, Amma. Be brave. Don't commit this sin,' he had begged her.

'Come and sit with us, Amma,' the children invited her. She blushed. Eagerness flashed in her eyes. The man grabbed the axle and stopped the carousel.

'Come, ammini. Come and sit here.'

'But I am not a child!'

'Everyone becomes a child when they sit on this ride, ammini!'

Very reluctantly, she mounted a horse and seated herself. The horse buckled, unable to bear her weight. It turned its head to give her a pitiable look and then stood perfectly still. The carousel man gasped too, trying strenuously to make the carousel go round but in vain. Why, they were heavy as corpses! The crowd of onlookers couldn't contain their laughter when they saw the carousel man standing helpless, with his eyes about to pop from the strain.

'Why don't I get down?' she asked shyly.

'There is no need. I am strong enough.'

He slapped his own shoulders. It was a challenge for him. He held his breath and pulled the lever. The axle shook. His shoulders flexed. Eyes squinted. Veins bulged. 'Hoye!' he shouted and kicked the ground with his feet. The carousel's horses neighed, straining under their load. Then the carousel yielded. It began to move slowly, like a mammoth lizard. The children leapt with joy. Sitting on a wooden horse, she too revolved towards her childhood. The carousel began to rotate fast, extending its canopy to the limit. The children yowled, overcome with delight.

She too had ridden a carousel like this in her childhood. In size, it was less than a third of this one. Even that one had made her head spin. She would cry, not wanting to ride. But her brother would insist and make her get on the carousel. As soon as the carousel began to spin, she became cheerful. Her brother would stand below and watch her fly like a bird with her wings aloft. Perched on the horse, she would laugh at him. The train of boxes turning smoothly and then sliding as if to bump into him before they passed, unnerved her brother. Later, it became a craze for her. Just as she had been addicted to the forest and its butterflies, she also grew infatuated to the carousel.

The children raised an ear-splitting din.

For the children, used to wandering inside a forest for ages, the carousel was a source of boundless joy. She felt that she had committed the sin of snatching away their childhood from them. She wondered whether, instead of heading to that abandoned well inside the forest, she could have done something else. She could have gone to some distant, anonymous place and raised them to adulthood with her hard work.

A large crowd had gathered to gawk at them riding the carousel.

'Look at these children, so pretty they're sure to attract the evil eye!'

'Their mothers will perform drishti for them tonight to ward it off!'

'All seven of them look so alike! As if they were born to the same mother!'

'There! The woman who's sitting on the horse must be their mother. Look at the children. They look exactly like her, exactly from the same mould.'

'They don't look like they belong to this area. Even their complexion is not typical of this place!'

'Look at the posture of the boy sitting on that horse, like Raja Desingu! There is such a regal lustre on his face!'

'She, too, carries herself like a queen.'

'She must be a queen of the jungle. Look at what she's wearing!'

'She smells of the wild animals in the forest!'

'No, it is the smell of parrots!'

'And the children smell of pigeons!'

'Who can they be?'

Nallaal became nervous. Was the village about to discover her and her children?

'Tell your children to get down, ammini. It's been a while since the carousel stopped. There are people waiting for the next round.'

With the help of the eldest sibling, the other children got off the carousel. The carousel man extended his hand to help Nallaal dismount. Ignoring him, she jumped down. The carousel man's face fell.

'You won't get polluted, ammini. A carousel operator is equal to god. All right, give me the fare. You and your seven children make eight. For eight riders at one anna per head, it will be eight annas!'

He started leading the customers by the hand to help them mount the horses for the next round.

Nallaal was distraught.

'But I don't have any money!'

He laughed.

'Just because I said that the carousel operator is equal to god, does it mean that you shouldn't pay? Even a carousel man has a stomach to feed. He can't turn this wheel on a hungry stomach, ammini. Stop playing games and pay up. There are people waiting!'

'Not at all. I don't know how to play games. I am standing here empty-handed!' She was contrite. The carousel operator became angry. 'Then you shouldn't have got on the ride. Did you come here with your children to seek alms? I don't have the means to give you alms, ammini. If you spend your life's breath turning and turning this axle, you'll know what the effort is worth. Come, grab this lever and turn it for one round. When you finish, your debt will be repaid. Come, ammini.'

Pulling her sari tight between and around her legs, she went under the canopy. When she grabbed the lever, her eldest boy stood in her way.

'Let me turn it, Amma!'

'No, my boy. You're not strong enough.'

The boy laughed.

'Who told you? Have you tested my strength? You think I am still a child, don't you? Give me a chance. Just stand over there and see how strong I am. You too, carousel owner! No one else should stand near the lever!'

There was indescribable contempt on the carousel owner's face. He exited the canopy and came outside. Standing with his hands folded across his chest, he prepared to watch the proceedings. She too left the canopy. The boy laughingly grabbed hold of the lever. It was too big for his hands. She was miserable. Tears welled up in her eyes. As if he was hugging a wooden toy-figurine, her boy hugged the carousel's axle. Holding a spoke of the canopy, he hoisted himself up to stand on the lever's stick. He kicked the lever with his tender feet. The carousel began to turn. The riders on the horses were taken aback. The carousel owner's eyes grew wide in amazement. The carousel, which revolved with the gurgling sounds of a mountain stream, gathered speed. The children roared. There was great dismay on the faces of those who stood around the carousel.

'Is this really happening? I just can't believe it!'

'This child couldn't have been weaned properly yet!'

'I see the Lord of Pazhani in him! How can an ordinary mortal to do such things!'

Unable to withstand the speed of rotation, the horses fell silent. Those seated on the horses shut their eyes tight. Nallathangaal was proud beyond words. The carousel owner, stunned at first, recovered soon.

'That's enough, boy! Your account is settled. There are people waiting for the next round.'

The boy emerged smiling from under the canopy.

'Which account are you talking about, carousel man?'

'The debt you owed me is paid up!'

After replying, the carousel man tried to spin the canopy. He began to pant.

'I'll give you a hand if you want,' the boy stepped forward. 'Why don't you rest for a while, carousel man?'

The carousel man was amazed.

'If only I had a son like you…' With a sigh he abandoned the lever and came out.

'Carousel… carousel!' Calling people to the ride like a seasoned professional, the boy climbed the lever and stomped on it. His mother was elated that he had mastered the technique in such a short time.

'We are hungry, Amma. Can't we find any fruits here?' cried the children. She didn't know.

The carousel man, who was standing nearby, was very kind. 'I'll be right back,' he said and returned with snacks.

'My darlings, eat up. All these are for you!'

The children ate greedily.

'Why don't you eat too, ammini? Don't you feel hungry? It's night already!'

'Never mind,' she declined.

'Eat, ammini. Don't feel shy. Your face looks sallow!'

Then, yielding to his insistent demand, she ate a few.

IV

Over time, she became the carousel woman. They had a cart for carrying the carousel and two bulls. In the manner of birds, the carousel man knew all about the coordinates of villages where festivals were held and the corresponding seasons. He didn't have a home or native village. Apart from the carousel which fed him and a hand-drum, he had no other possessions. He had been apprenticed to this vocation since childhood. Apart from that, he told her nothing else. She, too, didn't have any other questions. When the festival was over and they were ready to leave, he invited her to bring her seven children and come with him. At first, she was angry.

'I didn't say anything wrong, did I, ammini? You are stranded along with these children, without a man to support you.'

She had nowhere to go. She thought of going back to the jungle, but her children did not want to. The world was a source of great wonder to them. Every human seemed like a miracle. Only the carousel man had any trace of the humans she had encountered ages ago. Like her, he too looked like an ancient man. His body was thin as a bird's, with hands outstretched like wings. There was a pheasant's odour on his hirsute body.

Very reluctantly, she climbed onto his cart. The eldest boy sat next to the carousel man and took the whip in his hand. The other children slept beside her, hugging the horses. When dawn broke, the cart stood on the outskirts of an unrecognizable town. It was in that town that she started her life as a carousel woman. The carousel man taught her what to do. She learned fast.

They reached a village or town at least two days before the commencement of the festival. It took them at least two days to clean the ground where the carousel was to be installed and for pitching a tent for the children to sleep in. She cooked food for him and the children and then went around the forest and riverbank in search of grass for the bulls. The responsibility of tending to the horses fell to the children. In the interval between one festival and another, they had to wash the horses and give them a fresh coat of colour, mend the broken stirrups and paint them. The children watched everything without blinking an eyelid. Then they fetched grass from the nearby forests for their pet horses and compelled the latter to eat.

V

One evening the carousel man brought two baby rabbits from the forest on the outskirts of the village for the children to play with. The children hooted with joy. All day long, the carousel man lounged about, happily drunk on toddy. She cooked rabbit stew especially for him.

'Have a little, ammini.'

'No,' Nallathangaal declined angrily.

'What's the problem, ammini? I haven't said anything wrong, have I?'

Then he took his udukkai – hand-drum – and went out of the tent. She listened to him play the udukkai as he sang. She couldn't understand the song's meaning, but she found the melody enormously moving. She went to sleep with tears in her eyes. In her dreams, she was besieged by memories of the past. Unable to bear their weight, she wept and wailed aloud. The carousel man flung his udukkai away and came running to her; he was taken aback.

'What happened, ammini?'

In a very hushed tone, she replied: 'I had a dream, a very old dream…!'

He sat beside her and wiped the tears streaming down her cheeks. To console her, he also tried to gently pat her hair. Enraged, she slapped his hands away. The carousel man was puzzled.

'Why are you so angry, ammini?'

Her eldest was inseparable from the carousel man. He taught the child the finer aspects of operating the carousel. In a very short time, the boy took over the entire responsibility of the carousel. She was amazed at the deftness with which he turned the carousel. She stayed awake every night and waited for him till he returned to the tent after the day's work. After he finished dinner and lay down to sleep, she would massage his legs. Her heart overflowed with love and care for the boy. 'Are you not finding it hard?' she would ask tenderly, caressing his innocent face with both hands. 'What hardship, Amma? My life has found a meaning only now. I am finally able to do something for you and my siblings. In fact, this is a boon for me!' the boy laughed. The carousel man bought brand new clothes for her and the children. The ruddiness of good health had begun to show on the children's bodies. Gradually those bodies grew plump and big. Except for the eldest boy, the others had lost their memories of the past. When Nallathangaal heard a child address the carousel man as father, she was upset. Raising funny sounds from his udukkai and telling them stories, the carousel man was keeping them happy.

A troupe of itinerant acrobats was travelling with them from town to town. A girl with a snake's body, a boy who walked a tightrope, an old man who swallowed hot coals, a youth who dragged a rock tied to a rope with his teeth, a glutton who swallowed a large measure of cooked rice and hundred bananas at the same time – all these and several more travelled along with them. The children liked the glutton very much. He would carry them on his back, pretending they were salt sacks. The carousel man compensated him by giving him plenty of snacks to eat. As a mother, Nallathangal was overjoyed at seeing her children's rapture.

One night the carousel man was playing his udukkai and singing outside the tent. Nallathangaal too came out of the tent to listen to his story.

Taken by surprise, the carousel man raised a happy new beat from his udukkai that spread all over her body. Unable to bear its magnetic pull, she became edgy. She was distressed to discover that her heart, which had stayed frozen for ages, was now bursting with excitement. Her arteries pulsed and her breathing became erratic. Sweat poured out of her like a fountain. Unable to stand it, she returned to the tent. The children were fast asleep. Like a deeply frightened person, she lay down and clung to her eldest son in a tight hug. Sensing the tremors of her body, the boy woke up. In the soft light of the chimney lamp, she saw the boy looking at her, his eyes full of sympathy. Scared to look into them directly, she lowered her head. Her body was heaving with sobs. The boy, who was looking at her, raised her face. 'Don't cry, Amma,' he wiped her tears. 'Forget everything, Amma. None of us needs to harbour memories of the past.' He gently leaned her on his chest.

Outside the tent, the carousel man's udukkai was summoning her relentlessly: 'Ammini! Ammini!'

VI

During a festival, Nallathangaal went with her children to visit a small zoo. The tiger in that zoo recognized her and the children. The animal, which had been staring intently at them from inside the cage, jumped out at an opportune moment. The spectators fled screaming. Without disturbing anyone, the tiger came straight to her. Like a pet puppy, it jumped on her and the children, and licked their hands. The children started playing with the tiger. Two of them sat on its back. Very happily, the tiger walked a few rounds carrying the children. The crowd, which had scattered and run pell-mell, looked on from a safe distance. Hearing the news, the carousel man also came there. After having watched the scene fearfully, with much hesitation he broached the topic later that night.

'Who are you, ammini?' What's that tiger to you?' he bombarded her with questions.

She managed to say something in reply. He seemed to be very frightened and didn't speak to anyone for four or five days. When she or one of the children approached him, he moved away testily. She was worried. She also wondered whether she should tell him who she was. She doubted that the world would believe her. She also worried that the carousel man might go away, leaving her and the children behind. She was also not sure whether they would be able to go back to the jungle. Would the children follow her as before? She was indeed pleased with the changes that had come over them. They had learnt to understand and struggle in the world.

The tiger had come when her memories were gradually fading away. The next day, the tiger escaped the cage and came to their tent. Sensitive to its smell, she came out of the tent. The tiger clung to her. She petted it by rubbing its skin. Then in very hushed tones, she pleaded with it to go back. With a heavy heart, the tiger took leave of her and went away.

Later one day, she saw an itinerant singer who looked like her brother among the festival crowd. The singer, who was stunned to see her, stopped singing. He kept his udukkai on the ground and stared at her intently in the light of surrounding torches. A look of greed flashed in his eyes. Was survival a lasting curse for him, too? Was he wandering in search of her? Had he come back to life in a new incarnation? She rose from the crowd in a disturbed state. When they saw her get up, her seven children rose too. The singer choked on seeing her walk away with her seven children, who followed her in single file. Then he played his udukkai with great fervour. 'Come, come,' the udukkai pleaded. 'Nalla, my golden child!' it wailed. Then: 'Nalla, my chaste jewel! Don't go away with that carousel man! The world will condemn you!' A great cry rose from his udukkai and pierced her eardrums.

Dragging her children with her, Nallathangaal ran headlong into the night.

When they were halfway to the tent, it started raining heavily. She was out of breath. Her mind was restless. 'God, what shall I do?' she groaned aloud as she reached the tent. Oblivious to the rain, the carousel man waited anxiously outside.

'What happened, ammini? What made you come running like this in the driving rain?' He hugged the children. 'Come, ammini. You are going to catch a cold.'

'Carousel man! Will you do me a favour?'

'What do you want, ammini? Just say the word. Why do you even have to ask?'

'I want to go away from this town right now.'

'Where, ammini? What's happened to you? Is it something that somebody said?'

'I must leave this town and go away this minute, carousel man.'

'Where, ammini?'

'Wherever. Some place where they don't know who we are!

Take me to a place across the oceans and beyond the hills, carousel man,' she wept brokenly and held his feet in supplication.

Then without a word, the carousel man began to dismantle the carousel in the rain. The eldest boy came to his assistance. She packed the objects inside the tent into a sack. The singer was spitefully playing his udukkai. 'Nalla. Don't reject my words and go away. You'll invite rebuke, Nalla! Don't take your children and push them into an abandoned well, Nalla.' The sound was approaching closer. Playing his udukkai, Nallaan gave them a chase. They rolled up everything and piled it onto the cart. Nallaal's eyes were streaming with tears. Panic writ large on the carousel man's face. He wasn't someone who couldn't understand the udukkai's phrases, after all! He lifted the children onto the cart at lightning speed. Nallathangaal leapt aboard and hid herself behind his shoulders. Twirling and laying his whip on the bulls, the carousel man drove them faster and faster. Crossing forests, mountains and the towns encountered en route, the bulls hurried on. The singer's udukkai beat pursued them over a long distance. For seven days, they had no food or drink. Stopping at the deserted edges of forests, they ate the fruit and tubers they found there to quell their hunger.

Then they arrived at a town that was very far away. A river flowed by the town. Beside the river was a mountain. It was a town that had plenty of festivals and celebrations. There were countless carousel operators on the river bank. Traders and rich men had got together to enjoy themselves. The carousel man felt it would be a suitable location for them. Nallathangaal agreed with him. At a far corner of the town, he built a beautiful tent for her and her children. Then he set out with the eldest boy in search of a suitable spot for setting up the carousel. They came back to the tent at midnight. Exhausted, he lay down as usual on a straw mat outside the tent and fell asleep instantly.

At midnight, it began to pour.

When the sound of rain woke her, she thought at once of the carousel man. She came out of the tent in alarm, and on looking at the man who lay drenched in the rain, felt a boundless grief. 'Aiyo, carousel man.' She called out to him and tried to wake him. He lay inert and immobile like a corpse. It could have been the fatigue of travel as well as the intoxication of toddy. Without a second thought, she carried him on her shoulders inside the tent. She wiped his drenched body with the end of her sari and waited with boundless compassion for him to open his eyes. It took three days. Till then, she waited beside him without food or sleep. When he woke up three days later and looked around uncomprehending, she gave him an invaluable kiss. In this way, she became the carousel woman. And her seven children became the carousel man's children.

VII

To her, life seemed very simple.

A moustache had begun to sprout on the eldest boy's face. The other children too had started to grow up. Bodies which had remained frozen for ages had now begun to put forth tender leaves. One day she was startled to find a few grey hairs on her head. In a way, it was a big relief. Didn't it signify freedom from the curse of being alive? She was breaking free even from ancient memories. Nallaan's image was finally fading from her consciousness. She had completely forgotten her husband's face. If they stood before her, she wouldn't even recognize them, she thought. Her body, which had reeked of the odour of jungle beasts, smelt now of the carousel man's sweat.

The carousel man, though, was growing younger by the day. In a way, she was a boon to him. In a few weeks, she became pregnant. She was happy to think of the unborn child as her eighth along with the seven she had. The carousel man wanted a girl. 'We need a baby girl, don't we?' Their wish came true at the end of ten months. After the birth of the baby girl, he became a highly responsible man. All the seven children were overjoyed. By turns, they carried the child on their shoulders. Holding the child, the carousel man wandered all over the forest and riverside.

Nallathangaal got used to her life as a carousel woman fairly quickly. Just as they had loved the carousel man, the townspeople began to love her too. They lovingly plied the carousel woman and her children with the eats they specially prepared for the festival. She learnt to receive them by spreading the end of her sari and to express her gratitude before taking her leave. She didn't feel bad about going out of her tent every day at the crack of dawn to someone's cattle shed in order to cadge a tumbler of cow's milk for her baby girl. The carousel man had built a small house in the fishermen's colony by the river for her and the children. When the children went out to play, the couple became children themselves. She laughed all the time. Sometimes she would choke from laughing continuously. The carousel man went a little crazy whenever he set eyes on his carousel woman whose body had not lost its firmness even after bearing eight children.

'It seems like you want another girl child?' she would wink at him mischievously.

'Yes. Another seven girls. Seven boys and seven girls.'

'Do you think we'll survive that?' she would laugh.

While she slept like an innocent after they were done with playing, the carousel man stayed awake gazing at her face. One night she woke up suddenly.

'What happened, carousel man? Can't sleep?'

He sighed.

'Carousel woman, will you stay with me till the end?'

'Why ask this question now, carousel man. Just go to sleep.'

'But I will have no life left without you and the children, carousel woman. I am so worried...'

'Why do you doubt it, carousel man? I'll be here with you to the end of my life!'

True to her word, she was spending her life with him, enduring countless hardships. But after many ages, famine returned to their land. The sky played false. The river went dry. The land was parched, turning into desert. The grass withered. Seeing their wooden horses wilt from hunger, the children wept and cried. She was distraught. From that riverbank where all celebrations had died down, people were migrating steadily. Their carousel lay baking in the sun, its axle broken. The carousel man foraged in the dry ground next to the riverbank for a few tubers and brought them to her children. The eldest boy caught rats hiding in the clefts between rocks and limpets capable of surviving the worst of famines. Everyone held on to their lives, eating what little they could find. Just as she herself had done many years ago, a woman killed herself by jumping into a dried up well with her four children. No one came looking for them. The town's peace was shattered by the ceaseless growls of animals that were eating those bodies to quell their hunger. Nallathangaal watched everything with sorrow.

'Carousel man, do you think we will make it?'

'Don't lose heart, carousel woman. It will rain soon. The famine will lift. There is strength left in my shoulders.'

From that day, the carousel man travelled to distant places looking for work and brought back the food grains he earned as wages for the hard labour of digging the ground and breaking rocks. He watched over her with relentless anxiety, even staying awake all night. He followed her on some pretext or other whenever she went out of the house. The king of that town had also made a few arrangements. He had opened water troughs and food hangars, enabling his subjects to eat at least a little gruel every day to assuage their hunger. She didn't mind having to wait long hours in front of the gruel trough with her eight children. Satisfied that her role as a mother had finally become meaningful, she fought the famine with determination. It was such a woman who was forced, unable to bear the cruelty of a word uttered by the carousel man, to go looking for that abandoned well.

VIII

By then the famine had passed and the festivities were back. Another boy had come to assist the eldest in turning the carousel. The other children were playing happily with the little baby girl. Nallathangaal felt happy watching the girl toddle all over the place, lisping seductively. The carousel man's udukkai leapt in ecstasy. Nights, the couple would turn into little children on the riverbank.

Intoxicated by toddy, he babbled: 'I want another baby girl, carousel woman!'

'Keep quiet, carousel man! As if eight children aren't enough! We have aged, too!'

'Not enough. The account isn't settled yet!'

'Which account, carousel man?'

'Have you forgotten what you had said? Seven boys and seven girls. So, we have six more to go!'

'Aiyo! I can't do it, carousel man! I don't have the strength.'

'Drink a little of this. You'll become strong,' the carousel man said, extending his bowl of toddy to her.

Occasionally, they quarrelled. Sometimes he even beat her. Then she became very angry. Until her anger subsided, she wouldn't even talk to him. She turned her face away, as though he was a stranger to her. But the carousel man couldn't bear being estranged for more than a few hours. He pleaded, apologized and kept circling her for mercy and forgiveness. But she would not yield. Then he wept and slapped himself on the face for having allowed the toddy to fog his brain. Their children tried to make peace between them. He would often send the fisherwomen from neighbouring houses as emissaries.

'Let it go, ammini. Poor carousel man hasn't had so much as a drop of water in three days!' There were fisherwomen to plead his case. Seeing his plight made her want to laugh. She concealed her amusement with difficulty. Then, at some random moment, peace would descend between them. But one night, she could not tolerate a word of abuse that he had flung at her during a quarrel.

It was the hour of night when he was drunk senseless on toddy. For some reason, he called her a whore. She was taken aback. She tried to retaliate by using a very weak word of abuse. He assaulted her with the same invective.

'Whore! Aren't you a whore? You bore seven children for someone else, and now you've delivered an eighth for me,' he shouted and began to laugh derisively at her. In that moment, she remembered the previous era of her life. She recalled the times when she had frolicked along with her brother in the forest during her childhood. Her marriage, which was celebrated with great fanfare to the envy of the whole town, rose in her memory. She remembered the times she spent in her in-laws' place, drenched in her husband's love. Then she recalled that cruel famine and that abandoned well. Nallaan had brought her back to life by sprinkling holy water on her. He invited her, along with her children, to accompany him. This is a curse, Anna, only a curse!

She didn't utter a word.

She walked briskly to her home. The boys were playing in front of the entrance. The eighth child was in her crib. The other children were playing with the wooden horses. With her hair dishevelled and loose, she went to her children and said, 'Come, let's go.'

The children looked at her uncomprehending.

The eldest boy asked: 'Where to, Amma?'

She was close to tears. 'To the forest.'

'To the forest or to the abandoned well, Amma?'

She stood holding the hands of her children. The eldest boy picked up the baby girl. They walked in silence. On the way, he plucked rosary peas from the creepers and stored them in his waist pouch. Once they reached the edge of the forest, he began scattering the peas as he walked.

'What are you doing?'

'The man to whom this child belongs has to find his way to her, hasn't he?' He pointed to the baby asleep on his shoulder. Then they walked in silence. When the goatherds wandering about in the forest saw them, a tremor of apprehension shook them.

'Why are you going this way, ammini, along with your children? Did the carousel man say anything to you?'

She didn't reply. The children were overjoyed to see the birds in the forest which appeared to be totally free. They walked relentlessly through night and day. The eldest boy plucked jamun fruit for everyone.

'You want roasted fruit or raw ones?' he asked his mother from the topmost branch of the tree.

'Roasted!' cried the children. The fruit fell to the ground in a shower. The children picked them up greedily and gathered them in a waist pouch. She refused to eat them.

At last they reached the abandoned well. There was plenty of water in it.

'Shall I jump in first, Amma?' the eldest boy asked her as he climbed up and stood on the well's dilapidated parapet.

'No. We will jump in together.'

One by one, they climbed up and stood on the parapet. She joined them last. Their reflections were visible on the clear expanse of water. She closed her eyes for a moment. It was then that she heard the carousel man's voice.

'Aiyo! What do you think you are doing, carousel woman! Why get so angry over a careless word uttered by a drunk! For that one word, must you come and stand here with your children, like Nallathangaal?'

Unable to bear it any longer, Nallathangaal turned towards him. The carousel man was never able to forget that look for the rest of his life.

Translated from the Tamil short story *Uyirthezhudalin Saabam* (2010).

Note: The story of Nallathangaal is a tragic folktale which is very popular in Tamilnadu. Although the story's main event is narrated as a tale, it is believed that Nallathangaal actually lived. It is said that, besieged by poverty and unable to bear her sister-in-law's harsh and cruel words, Nallathangaal killed her seven children by throwing them into a well and followed them into it to end her own life. Moved by the intolerable grief of her demise, her brother Nallathambi also jumped into the same well and killed himself.

In admiration for the exemplary affection between brother and sister, Sivan and Parvati appeared there and brought back to life not only Nallathangaal and her seven children, but also her brother, Nallathambi. Nallathambi and Nallathangaal then said, 'We are dead and let us remain dead. Let there not commence a history of those who were born as mortal human beings being resurrected after death. Grant in your mercy that we shall remain dead.' For this sole reason, Nallathangaal is worshipped as a deity in southern Tamilnadu.

A Place Called Home

Just as Seenu had said when he had come to visit him years ago, Chinnu's grandfather's house was in ruins, and in a far worse condition than reported by Seenu.

The sun had forced its way in through the collapsed roof. The walls had developed cracks, and the plaster had broken off in several places. Chinnu saw fat-bellied wood lizards clinging to the walls and tracking the visitors with their intimidating eyes. Scattered on the scarred and pitted floor were large piles of sparrow droppings. As soon as he opened the door, a host of small, frightened sparrows whirred up noisily and flew away in all directions. Unable to bear their stench, Maheshwari shut her nostrils tight. She had followed him in cautiously, but when she spotted the rotting corpse of a snake curled up in an alcove, she stepped back in alarm. As she rushed back to the entrance, ranting incoherently, he noticed that a rope of cobweb had wound itself around her head. He picked up a stick lying near his feet, deftly rolled the snake's lifeless body onto it and came out of the house. The body was a mere skeleton. When he flung it on the fence knitted with Indian Balm trees, the cadaver snapped into two with a light sound and fell to the ground.

Maheshwari had taken refuge under the big tamarind tree at the entrance.

There were bunches of raw green fruit on its outspread branches that were as dense with leafage as bushes. Looking up at the tree's giant shape, she saw the round eyes of a large-winged black bird staring intently at her from one of its topmost branches. She was frightened. When he saw her eyes brimming with tears, Chinnu became very angry. He found a sharp-edged stone on the ground and flung it at the bird, which was sitting perfectly still. Unbelievably, the bird dropped straight down from the branch and fell at her feet with a soft thud. She picked up the bird in her hands. Its weightless body was totally dry. At the touch of her hand, its feathers disintegrated into tiny bits which began to float in the air around her. After throwing away that carcass in disgust, she sat down dejectedly on a slab of granite lying under the tree.

Chinnu lit a beedi and sat down on his haunches in front of her. She seemed unwilling to look at his face. He was unable to say a single word to console her. He saw several red ants crawling near her feet. He was worried: what would they do if those ants bit her? He stood up, wary that warning her about them might worsen her mood. 'Watch where you sit. There are plenty of red ants here. They can bite you,' he told her casually.

Walking to the entrance without any hint of anxiety, he entered the abandoned house. On the pitted, uneven floor, there was a pile of broken tiles. A lizard with a bloated belly peeped out from an anthill in a corner and then scurried to hide. Crawling freely everywhere until then, the wood lizards were in a sudden panic. They jumped on the yellowing walls and moved very swiftly towards the roof. Chinnu stood still for a few minutes, listening to the sighs they exhaled through the holes in the dried up bamboo rafters. When he tapped the middle of a bamboo rod with the tip of his iron sickle, the small creatures went quiet immediately and hid themselves. Plaster had come off at many spots on a wall, making it look grotesque. But the walls of that house, which must have been sixty or seventy years old, were very strong. If its roof hadn't collapsed, this house wouldn't have been so badly ravaged, thought Chinnu. Then he began to carefully inspect every room in the house. It was the front hall which had suffered the most severe damage. Along the wall was a rat's burrow with a little pile of excavated mud next to it. A rat or bandicoot must be living there, he thought. The bamboo rafters holding up the roof seemed to be still sturdy. Many of the battens had become weak. That must be the main reason for the collapse of the tiles, he thought.

He hesitated briefly before touching the door that separated the front hall from the main house. After wiping away the thick layer of dust on the picture of Murugan that his grandfather had pasted over the intricately carved figures on the door, he discovered that its lustre was more or less intact. When his grandfather cut that picture out of a calendar and pasted it on the door forty years ago, he was a little boy standing next to him. When that moment came back to him with acute clarity, he became edgy. A few days later, he had pasted a photo of MGR on that door. He had cut the photo out of a book he had found in his uncle's house. His grandfather was not at home at the time. His mother had gone to the well to draw water. Exactly when he entered his grandfather's room to look for the bottle of gum to paste the picture, his mother returned home. By the time he heard the sound of her slippers at the entrance, he had already found the bottle of gum and returned to the front hall with his right index finger dipped in gum. He sat leaning against the wall, diligently applying gum on the back of the MGR photo. Once his mother went away after checking on him, he pasted it six inches above the portrait of Murugan. It was a very small photograph, but his grandfather spotted it very easily. The old man was furious. He tried everything he could to tear it off the door. He even succeeded to an extent. But MGR's forehead and eyes, along with his upper lip and a portion of his moustache and neck, were stuck so firmly that they could not be torn off. Fearful of his grandfather's wrath, he ran away and hid himself in Pottuchami temple. Many hours later, his mother came there looking for him. A small scrap of that photo was still stuck to the door.

Chinnu tugged and pulled back his corpus of memories from their attempt to enter the dark-infested snake-pit of time; he thought instead about the repairs to be done on the house. His first task was to sweep away the large mounds of sparrow shit which seemed to be everywhere, along with the dirt and dust. Starting six or seven months ago, he had thought a lot about the dilapidated condition of the house and considered what was needed to restore it. After having spent most of his life till then in a prison cell, he received a substantial amount of money from the jail administration as wages for the work he had done. As soon as Maheshwari heard his idea of returning to this house, she told him that it would be in ruins. She was the one who instilled in him the hope that they would be able to renovate the house without anyone's help. He told her that in his prison term of fourteen years, he had acquired all the skills necessary for renovating a house and showed her his calloused hands. They bought a spade, crowbar and a sickle with a pointed tip, and reached the abandoned house. They were surprised to find that everything they had left behind was lying safe and undisturbed.

Because they were scared of him, the people of his village had not touched anything in the house during his absence. In the dust-coated kitchen, utensils covered by the verdigris of time lay scattered in all corners. Many vessels were made of brass and bronze. There were rotting eggshells inside a copper container filled with the carcasses of lizards. The time they were away must have brought a spirit of revelry to these small creatures, he thought.

Not one of the coconut trees, which had formed spathes by the time he left, was still alive. But under the sangam bushes which had proliferated into a thick jungle, the well dug by his grandfather was safely hidden. Chinnu took the brand new sickle in his hand. Wrapping her sari tight and tucking the free end at her waist, Maheshwari stood ready assist him. He climbed the Portia tree still standing by the fence with its pride intact, and cut a sturdy forked stick for his use. When he straightened up after hacking and clearing the kundali bushes which had completely blanketed the water surface, he was breathless. Kneeling at the well's edge, he bent down and scooped up the brimming water in both hands and gave it to her. She slid the handful of water into her mouth as if it was holy. 'Sweet as sugarcane. After so many years, the taste has remained the same!' Amazed, she wet her hands by dipping them in the expanse of water. When she touched the surface densely covered with moss, it gave her gooseflesh. Dangling his legs in the cold water, he closed his eyes. A shoal of carp swarmed in to nibble at his cracked soles. When he saw a black shadow which had started to climb slowly from the bottom of the well, he stood up hastily. Flapping its fins, it swam up and stood with its head raised above the water and mouth open. This was his grandfather's swordfish, a creature awaiting his return. He stripped a handful of knotgrass flowers from a nearby plant and scattered them on the water surface. The swordfish swam up greedily and devoured the flowers; then it spat them out in disappointment and disappeared into the depths of the water. In another room, his grandfather's rope-cot of many years lay untouched. But its frayed ropes, which had dropped to the floor, lay all over the house like dead snakes. He concluded that that everything they had left behind was most likely still safe and intact.

They might even use a few of those objects which had withstood the ravages of time. Reminding himself that nothing good could ever come out of such fantasies, he fetched Maheshwari and started consulting her about repairs to the house. She was upset on seeing the house in such a terrible state. Saying that it would be impossible for him to repair the house on his own, she suggested that he call someone to assist him. Unable to reject her suggestion, he went to his orchard on the far bank of the river in search of Seenu. When he saw revulsion for him crawling like caterpillars on the wrinkled faces of Seenu's aged parents, Chinnu came away without asking them anything. It was the barber Ponga Navidan, sitting alone on the riverbank with his box of shaving paraphernalia, who had warned him about the town's hatred. The ancient, ravaged barber with his shrunken eyes could not recognize him initially. When he did, his body started to shiver in fright. He wept for a long time thinking about all the ignominy Chinnu's grandfather had put up with just to earn his livelihood. Then, with unbearable sorrow, he shut his mouth with a towel. Even long after Chinnu had left, the barber kept repeating over and over again, 'It's fate, sami, just fate.' When Chinnu returned, feeling extremely weary, to that ruined house, Maheshwari gave him a bronze pot filled with cold water from the well. Kitchen utensils glittered from the touch of her hand. 'What happened?' she asked him and without expecting a reply, turned stiffly like a wooden toy and went back to work. She had improvised a stove with three bricks under the tamarind tree and started cooking on it. In that village, which bore him a grudge, no one would be around to welcome them. Surely this could not be beyond her comprehension, he thought. He had forgotten many of the faces here. Even those he remembered would have dated back fifteen years. For a long time afterwards, he was unable to forget the rancour evident on those faces which had surrounded him as he was being pushed into the police van, his face swollen from being beaten by the police.

'Get in, punk! One slap is enough to make your eyes pop out!'

Those who had gathered to gawk at him ran away frightened. He heard someone laughing really loud. I'll never come back to this village, he swore to himself, and shut his eyes. When his grandfather passed away, he was permitted to go on parole to cremate him. But he turned it down. A few years later, he received the news that his mother had died. He hadn't known about it until Seenu came and told him. His eyes welled up when he heard about it. What hurt him more than his mother's death was the fact of being shunned by his relatives, who had not bothered to inform him. Seenu was calmly watching the teardrops roll down Chinnu's cheeks. Later, Seenu consoled him by suggesting that his relatives might not have told him because it would have upset him greatly. In the initial years of his term, Seenu visited him once a month without fail. It was Seenu who had told him that Maheshwari was involved with someone else. He listened to the news calmly. He also tried not to give it much credence. He thought his equanimity would have disappointed Seenu, who probably expected him to fly into a rage. He promised Seenu that he would ask her the next time she visited him.

But he was never able to ask her about it.

Maheshwari visited him every month without fail. From his vantage behind prison bars, he had closely observed the changes that were occurring in her body. Sometimes she appeared enervated, with her thin body, sunken eyes and dark skin. At such times, she wept for a very long time. She answered his questions heaving a deep sigh. At other times, she seemed to be in robust health. There were six or seven periods when she had not visited him for two or three months at a time. He imagined that she could be pregnant and was staying away only to hide it from him. However, she would arrive on a day when he was least expecting her. In the very short time that they were allowed, she tried to tell him about her troubles which he could never comprehend. Later, when it was nearly time for her to leave, amid threats and warnings from jailers that went rolling behind each visitor's back, she would enquire, in an unclear and agitated voice, about the years still left for his release. When the question came up without fail every time she took her leave, he could never face it without feeling agitated. While he was still thinking seriously over the question which he could never understand, leave alone answer, she would be sent out.

A few years ago, she suddenly stopped coming to the jail to visit him. He wondered if she had eloped with her lover. It gave him intolerable grief. He tried to console himself by concluding that she couldn't have acted differently. Grievance and ill-will against her grew in his heart. Once I am free, I must hunt her down wherever she may be and wreak vengeance, he decided. But when he realized that this was still several years away, he was depressed. He also pondered whether there was any way to escape from the prison. Day after day, he spent all his waking hours exploring the possibilities of staging a jailbreak. Several ideas occurred to him on how to test the strength of the bars in the mosquito- and cockroach-infested cell where he was locked up and on capturing the key for the lock on its door. While he was engaged in performing back-breaking tasks in the prison compound, his mind was invaded by speculations about the height of the surrounding wall, lined at the top with shards of glass and rings of electrified barbed wire, and fantasies about leaping over it and getting away, making him feel troubled and restless.

He was constantly disturbed by visions of Maheshwari lying with some other man. He imagined the other person to be a robust man. A tall and well-built man. He was probably fairer than Chinnu. He could even be a young lad who had just sprouted a moustache. The young man would have succeeded very easily in making the juices of love flow again in Maheshwari's parched body, Chinnu thought. His fantasies about their wallowing in pleasure every night grew and grew. Pictures of Maheshwari embracing that sturdy youth with unbridled lust would appear in disjointed fashion. Then his penis grew erect. Inside his filthy shorts made of tough fabric, it trembled like a frightened bird. Careful not to allow signs of that tremor to spread to the mouldering bodies of other prisoners who slept around him, he would try to calm its agitation. Later one night, the lifer who was sleeping next to him had found out about the secret of his tremors. That man's ruthless body got on top of Chinnu without any kind of hesitation. In the depths of his heart, a tiny spark of resistance rose and then subsided. Huddling like a young chicken under the man's body which reeked of a wildcat's stench, Chinnu got through that sad, loathsome experience. Lice falling from that man's hirsute body were crawling hungrily over Chinnu's sweat-soaked skin. Drops of that man's semen which flowed down the folds of his groin were spreading an unbearable rank smell in that room where the ruined and deformed bodies of another fifteen prisoners slept. A few prisoners who couldn't stand the stench turned over in their sleep. A young man who was a brand new entrant to the room coughed incessantly. An old codger who had been fast asleep woke up and looked around, blinking uncomprehendingly. The jailer dragged his stick across the metal bars, warning them with its rolling clangs, and then he was gone.

He couldn't even identify the man. He sat thinking about it till late at night. Then he remembered Maheshwari's body with its petals of lust unfurled. As he dwelt on her voluptuous breasts, plump thighs and hairy vagina, he tried to go to sleep. Years ago, he had retrieved the wonderful fragrances of lust from the pollen dust of her naked body and spread them all over the now ruined house of his grandfather. At the end of their first intercourse, the house was filled with the fragrance of screw pine leaves. He pulled her to him and asked her in a hoarse whisper if she was wearing screw pine leaves in her hair. She said no; then she whispered into his ear that she was intoxicated by the odour of crow-pheasant emanating from his body. But the fragrance of screw pine leaves was growing unbearably strong. His mother, who was fast asleep on a rope-cot in the anteroom, woke up, unable to bear the intensity of that fragrance. After raising the lantern's flame, she carried it to their bedroom, making strange sounds on the way to warn them of her arrival. Once there, she called her daughter-in-law who was lying on the bed with her clothes in disarray and asked her if she was wearing screw pine leaves in her hair. Even as Maheshwari was replying, Chinnu's grandfather who had been ailing and bedridden for long years woke up and came there. Chinnu's mother asked the old man if he got up and came there because he couldn't stand the scent of screw pine leaves. He nodded. The stiffness of his body had scared her. They asked one another whether there could be some screw pine leaves somewhere in the house. His grandfather who had lived there for a very long time replied that there was no chance of that. His mother went close to her daughter-in-law who was standing there with her body shaking in embarrassment and while stroking her hair, told her the answer to the riddle: 'Soon, very soon, my grandson will be born smelling of screw pine leaves!' she cried exultantly as she hurried away. His grandfather muttered the name of their clan deity in a burst of gratitude and left. Maheshwari covered her face, which had turned the ripe colour of shame, and lay face down on the bed. Chinnu tried to turn her over on her back and part her fingers for a look at her face. She, however, spurned him violently.

Early next morning, Chinnu got up in a panic on hearing the jailer's whistle and tried to spot the man who had scattered drops of semen in the folds of his crotch. Everyone had dispersed by then. A few days later, Chinnu was sent to a fellow prisoner to work as a carpenter's assistant. That rancorous man kept swearing at Chinnu and other assistants with the most horrible words of abuse. When Chinnu dared to butt in with a word of protest, the carpenter grabbed him by the hair on his closely cropped head and shook it fiercely. He gathered the saliva in his stinking mouth and spat directly on Chinnu's face. Chinnu did not speak a word after that. That very night, with the warden's connivance, the man had Chinnu transferred to the cell where he was locked up. When he got on top of Chinnu later that night, Chinnu resisted violently. But that man was far more aggressive than Chinnu. His penis penetrated Chinnu's buttocks in the most disgusting way. Chinnu tried to shout. However, when he remembered that it was a futile gesture, he decided to allow that man to bugger him. Chinnu's limp and flaccid penis must have angered that man. He grabbed Chinnu's penis and started to pull at it roughly. It was very painful for Chinnu, who began to screech like a hen. A prisoner who was sleeping beside them turned over in his sleep. Another prisoner began to cough. One of them sat up and blinked uncomprehendingly. The jailer's stick passed across the bars of the cell, creating a series of clanging sounds. Ignoring the noise, the man took Chinnu's limp penis in his mouth. Chinnu visualized Maheshwari's body, which always smelt of screw pine leaves. A hazy image that resembled someone else appeared in his mind. Then he tried hastily to imagine the naked shapes of all the girls he had fucked till then. As soon as he visualized a body with big breasts and a fat behind, his penis began to grow erect. Many years ago, he had spent a night with a whore who had a body like that.

Then he tried not to think of Maheshwari, to erase her from the screen of his memory. The female bodies that he remembered were also fading away, one by one. Lust for male bodies began to infect and spread in his veins with the intensity of a killer virus. He got used to loving the stench-filled nights. He yearned for them. When he fell roughly on the bodies of newly arrived prisoners who lay beside him, he began to think of himself as a totally free man. Through dominating weak bodies which lacked the strength to resist him, he felt that his empty heart was being filled with a mysterious sense of freedom. Sometimes he remembered that he had no relationship with anyone outside the prison bars. He was worried that when he was released, he might be stranded helpless in a deserted world. Whenever he had a chance to speak to the jail authorities, he would ask them if his term was going to end soon. Thoughts of leaving that familiar situation left him in turmoil. One officer had somehow understood his fears. One day, when that officer was relaxing under the ponga tree in the jail compound, Chinnu started chatting with him. When he learnt from the conversation that his release would take several years more, he felt relieved. In the remaining years he learnt many trades. During those years when nobody came to see him, he worked variously as sweeper, carpenter, construction worker, weaver, farm labourer and cook. Then he was appointed as the warden. His fellow prisoners treated him with respect. He was served an extra cup of tea in the morning. On occasion, he was given booze and ganja as well. He would request the jail authorities to allot the younger ones among the newly arrived prisoners to his cell. The authorities accepted his request with a smile and a wink. Nearly all such prisoners were stubborn and unyielding at first. Feeling humiliated and guilty, they swore at him. But once they realized that this was unavoidable for a male prisoner, they calmed down. Spraying his stinking semen in their groin folds and infesting their bodies with lice had become an intoxicating addiction for him. Fully experiencing the freedom of irresponsibility, he even forgot that he was sentenced for life and locked up in a prison cell.

Four or five years later, when he received word that a visitor had come to see him, he was stunned. There were tears in his eyes even before he reached the visitors' hall. As soon as he set eyes on her emaciated form, he began to wail loudly. He was very moved when she consoled him. When she begged his forgiveness for not having visited him in so many years, he was upset. He tried to tell her that it was not a problem at all. But she continued to beg his forgiveness. And he asked her repeatedly why she had become so thin and emaciated. She kept on insisting that he should tell her why his eyelids were swollen. By then their time was up and he had to go back. That night, he was sobbing for a very long time. When a fellow prisoner complained that it was disturbing him, he passed the night shedding tears in silence.

Then she came to visit him nearly every month. With every visit, he felt that her body was growing more beautiful. He liked to imagine that her young body was waiting for him. He tried to give up alcohol and ganja, little by little. But he couldn't give up exchanging bodily pleasures with other prisoners. During those times, he wanted to visualize Maheshwari's body.

But the moment her face appeared in his mind, his penis became limp. The harsh stench of disgust began to lay siege to him. The warm body lying in his embrace moved away from him in frustration and disdain. Once again, prison life turned intolerable for him.

Later, he began to dream about his release from prison and beginning a new life. He started to spend a lot of time mentally calculating the amount that would have accrued in his account as wages for the work he had done in the jail. The days inched very slowly over the prison cells enclosed within those large, rugged and frighteningly high compound walls. Each passing day tested the limits of his patience. One hot summer afternoon, the jail superintendent summoned him suddenly. Wiping his sweat-streaked face with his hands, Chinnu stood submissively in front of the superintendent, who smiled kindly at him. After informing him that he would be freed in exactly a week, the superintendent asked him if he was ready for it. Chinnu was overwhelmed. He wondered in confusion whether he should tell the other prisoners, but he couldn't arrive at an answer, so he spent that whole night without a wink of sleep. When he told Maheshwari who came to visit him two days later, she smiled without saying anything. A kind of panic flitted across her face, he thought. As though she had run out of her stock of words, she spoke very tersely and left in a hurry. He gave away the cheap sweetmeats that she had thrust into his hands to his comrades and lay down to sleep that night without eating anything. He spent the remaining hours of the night wondering whether she would come back to take him with her, concluding gloomily that it might have been their final meeting. But when he saw her shape fidgeting restlessly in the visitors' hall well before the assigned hour, he felt ashamed of having doubted her sincerity. After the rituals of his release were completed, the jail snapped its longstanding relationship with Chinnu and evicted him through a small back entrance. She took his hand in hers as if to console him, give him hope and share her happiness. He noticed that her eyes had welled up. She looked exhausted. The terror of uncertainty had spread around her melancholy eyes, which were red from lack of proper sleep. She was wearing an inexpensive sari that didn't look all that old. The string of flowers she wore in her hair was beginning to wilt. Her forehead was adorned with sacred ash and vermillion. She must have visited some temple before coming here, he thought.

She wanted to leave that place immediately, it seemed. As he was gazing distractedly at the high compound walls of the prison, she tapped his shoulder and said, 'Hurry!' to move him along. She trotted quickly ahead in order to get away from the stink of sweat from those bodies gone limp from waiting and being watched all the time and from their lugubrious voices. He walked behind her, feeling ashamed that he was finding it difficult to keep pace with her. The sun was stinging hot. First she asked him if he wanted to go to an eatery; then, not bothering about the consent of someone who had just been released from frozen time and was struggling to encounter a present that had moved very far away from him, she hired an autorickshaw. The city had changed a lot. He watched with amazement the constant traffic of cars, buses and two-wheelers speeding to and fro on the broad avenues. The auto in which they were travelling stopped very far from the city's main arterial road in front of an eatery on a congested street. From the manner of her taking leave of the auto driver, he suspected that he must have known her from before. The waiters at the eatery as well as the fat man who sat at the cash counter seemed to know her. She even attempted to introduce some of them to him. 'My husband,' she told them. Some smiled. A young man with frizzy hair took Chinnu's hand

and shook it. A middle-aged man just nodded at him and left. He found it strenuous to look at those men who had never lost their freedom or been accused of a crime.

Later, she led him down a narrow alley, past overflowing drains. A few people who passed them smiled at her. From her perch in front of a small house, an old, sickly-looking woman spat furiously when she saw them pass by. At the end of that path lined on both sides by huts, they came to an apartment block whose walls were moss-laden. She stopped. Wiping the flowing sweat on her face with the rolled up end of her sari, she started climbing up the narrow steps. She kept turning around often to check if he was following her.

As soon as the door was opened, they were assaulted by a rotten smell redolent of the stench that emanated from brown sheep drenched in the rain. Her house was just a hall measuring around a hundred square feet. It was even smaller than the cell in which he had been locked up for years. A mat and a couple of filthy pillows lay next to the wall. She dragged the mat to the centre and asked him to sit down. A calendar whose leaves had turned brown and a small framed picture hung on the greasy, brown walls. A few vessels, along with a kerosene stove, lay in a corner of the house. In another corner, he found a few mangoes, almost rotten, in a cane basket. He picked up a mango. 'I survive on selling these,' she said and stood up. She kept the door ajar and was in the process of changing, removing her sari completely, when there was a knock on the door. Ignoring it, she continued to change, when Chinnu got up and opened the door. He found an unfamiliar person standing there. 'Mages isn't home?' the man asked. Chinnu stood staring at him as though he didn't know the answer. She hurried to his side. 'My husband,' she told the visitor. The man smiled. Then he told her something in a hushed whisper. After he left, she latched the door. Exhausted from the day, Chinnu stretched out on the mat. She lay down close to him.

She got up very early every morning, well before Chinnu, cooked some food for him and then set out carrying the fruit basket. She seemed to be bereft of any hope that his arrival would bring about some change in her life or of any intention to change the conditions of her life. Left alone for the day after she went out, he would open the door and step out very hesitantly onto that noisy street. He would mostly pass women quarrelling fiercely, plastic containers aloft in their raised hands, around a municipal water truck, or children blocking the road as they played, and reach a wayside stall. After drinking a cup of tea there, he would buy two bundles of beedi and return home. On most days, Maheshwari returned home just after sunset with the unsold fruits in the basket, along with their nauseating smell. She was startled at the charred beedi stubs lying scattered all around the mat. Then she silently swept them up, cleaned the floor and got ready to cook. He did not ask her anything. Whenever he thought of her, he was overcome with guilt. She must have moved to the city where he was imprisoned solely for his sake. She wouldn't have had any reason to continue living in their village either. He followed the movements of that emaciated body with increasing dismay. Even when he gave her the money he had received from the prison as wages, her face remained impassive. She kept the money in her hand for a long time. After counting it two or three times, she put the money away safely in her old trunk and locked it. Her mind, which had lost all hope, was floating adrift like a withered brown leaf, thought Chinnu. He was determined to retrieve the founts of love once again from the depths of her parched and fissured body. One night when she was fast asleep, he embraced her lustily. As drops of sweat had begun to break out on her skin, his nostrils grew stiff and alert. When that horrible stench from his cell, which had stalked him all along like a spy, began to pervade that small house, his penis lost its tumescence. Only then did he remember his grandfather's house. He also recalled the fragrance of screw pine leaves which had wafted in during their first time together.

While he was walking alone with her down the foot trail filled with the reek of wild flowers, Chinnu asked her about the scent of screw pine leaves that had invaded his grandfather's house years ago. She looked up at him in confusion. As she thought of the crow-pheasant's odour emanating from his body, bashfulness flitted like a butterfly across her sweat-lined face. The house is probably in ruins, he thought for the very first time. Anxiety caught hold of him with its beak, like a kingfisher. When he saw his grandfather's house rise before him like an enormous jungle, he was stunned.

His muscles had grown strong with the hard labour of many years. He stood before the abandoned house like a tough and violent animal. After girding his loins with his veshti, he climbed onto the roof with a leap. That decrepit house groaned, unable to bear his weight. Like an expert carpenter, he checked the strength of the bamboo rafters very carefully. She was amazed at the deftness with which he dismantled the tiles and split the rafters. Rolling the end of her sari into a cushion on her head for carrying loads, she stood ready to assist him. A jungle crow which was disturbed by the smoke rising from the charred remains of firewood in the stone stove took fright and flew away with repeated cries of 'krav, krav', like a death lament. Villagers who happened to pass by that ruined house could scarcely believe their eyes. They rushed off with their nervous bodies to give the news to others. When the day began to shed its leaves one by one, Chinnu climbed down from the roof, proud of having cleared a small space in his grandfather's abandoned house for them to spend the night in. Maheshwari touched him with her thin hands and called him to eat. 'Wait. I'll bathe first. I am feeling sticky all over,' he said and went to the well.

'It'll be dark soon. If you want, I'll heat some water for you. You might catch a cold from bathing in cold water.' She followed him to the well. By then, he had already worn a loin cloth and jumped into the water. Still and quiet for so many years, the well greeted him with dismay. Erupting joyfully, the water dashed against the wall, broke into drops and slid back into the well. Cleaving the water with his strong arms, Chinnu swam towards the depths. The swordfish, stranded alone for so many years, took fright and went into hiding; after recognizing who he was, it swam over, flapping its fins, rubbed against him and moved away. 'You climb in, too. The water's nice and cold,' he stood on the bottom ledge and called her. 'No. There's water on the stove for me. Bathing in cold water at this hour will be unbearable,' she said and retreated into the house. Lighting a small earthen lamp, she lit a feeble flame in that ruined house. 'You have a bath, too. I've kept water for you at the door,' he told her. While he looked on in amazement at the flame of the earthen lamp which was flickering like a tiny, animate creature in that dilapidated house, she walked to the door. He looked at the roof of that abandoned house which was beginning to recover from its ruined state. It made him think up an enigmatic statement of hope. He came to the entrance, wanting to share it with her.

By then she had taken off all her clothes. The nakedness of the female body, which had been erased completely from his memory, gave him a jolt. He was overwhelmed. He felt breathless. His body trembled. When she turned in his direction by chance, bashfulness lit up her face like a small flame. Overcome by lust, he rushed to her and dragged her like a prey into the house. When he licked the drops of sweat on her skin, the sluice gates of lust, which had been silted up in his body, opened. She trembled at his aggression. The stiffness of refusal was evident in her body. She covered her still-wet breasts with her thin hands. He tried to remove her hands and grab them. She turned over and lay face down. He tried to penetrate her with his hard penis and open the founts of desire in her body. She moaned. It was then that he remembered the body of the prisoner who had got on top of him for the very first time. He tried to ignore the memory. His grandfather's house, which was emerging from its dilapidated state, was being pervaded by a stomach-turning odour. His hands, which had grabbed her erect nipples, began to shake. His penis began to shrink.

The buds of carnal desire had begun to bloom in her body just then. She was stuck to him in embrace like a wood lizard. She could scarcely believe the slackness she sensed in his body. Stung by unbearable humiliation, he moved away and tried to cover his nakedness with his hands. Her body was heaving in front of him. As if he wanted to plunge that house, which had just been rescued from ruin, in darkness, he blew his hot breath on the earthen lamp's tiny flame and put it out. Ignoring the sound of her sighs, he walked out of that ruined house. He lit a beedi and filled his lungs, still scented by her naked body, with black smoke from its cheap tobacco.

This body was ruined; it had become irreversibly deformed. This weightless body from which life had been plucked out would henceforth be merely a burden to him. He could no longer remember his innocent childhood or his youth when he was immersed in the depths of pleasure. In his mind, from which the scent of the female bodies from his past had faded totally, only this horrible odour had survived. His condemned senses would never again imbibe the fragrance of screw pine leaves wafting from the petals of nudity that lay within a hand's reach. He would never be free of the prison cell he had been locked in by the curse of the stink emanating from the dried sperm that lay in the folds of his groin, like the disfiguring scars on a leper's body.

Then he remembered the bodies of his fellow prisoners who mounted him for years and the brutal rhythm of their movements. Then, incredibly, his penis began to grow erect. Lust turned into a malevolent beast which grabbed him like a prey and dragged him back into that ruined house. He imagined that small space he had retrieved in his grandfather's house to be a stinking cell occupied by fifteen rotting bodies. He fell like an animal on her naked body, which had been covered upto now by the dead carcasses of time. She, who had lain trapped in the prison of a nightmare, woke up startled. Then, in anticipation of the brutal movements of his metallic body reeking of a crow-pheasant's odour, she stripped her body of the cloaks of shame and laid herself open.

Translated from the Tamil short story *Veedenba* (2011).

In Conversation with Devibharathi
N. Kalyan Raman

Translator's Note

P.S.

Insights
Interviews
& More...

In Conversation with Devibharathi

N. Kalyan Raman

It took me more than six months to schedule an interview with Devibharathi, who had moved to his village near Erode in Tamilnadu earlier this year to devote himself to writing full-time. It was a chance literary assignment that brought him to Chennai in early August. He extended his visit by a day to make himself available for a conversation with me about his background, writing life, beliefs and social concerns. A slightly built, bespectacled man in his mid-fifties, Devibharathi wore a disarming smile as he answered my questions with coherence and fluency. Since I chose not to record the interview, preferring to work from notes, there were a couple of supplementary telephone calls to clarify a specific detail or to amplify a statement. I hope the interview presented here helps the reader understand the writer and his milieu, and sheds light on the many facets of his creation, the stories themselves.

N. Kalyan Raman (NKR): Can you describe your early encounters with books and literature? Who were your favourite writers at that time?

Devibharathi (DB): I was born and raised in a small village near Arachalur in Tamilnadu's Erode district. I was the third of five children in my family. As a young man, my father had fought in World War II. After the war, he took up a job as a teacher in a government school. His father, my grandfather, was also a school teacher. I was born in a household with a collection of around fifty books. We also bought the daily newspaper at home. So I grew up to become a regular reader very early in my life. The writers I admired in those days were Sandilyan and Akilan, who were very popular fiction-writers of the time. I read whatever I could lay my hands on. Writing came naturally to me. When I was still in highschool, I edited and produced a handwritten magazine, which I continued to bring out till the end of my school days. I also took part in writing competitions in school and won prizes. I grew up wanting to be like the writers I read avidly – popular and famous.

When I was in sixth standard, my father was suspended from his job. As a result, I had to stay back from school for two years because my family could not afford to pay the annual special fees. This happened once more, so I lost three years due to poverty. Finally, I took up a job selling eats at a movie theatre to earn enough money to see me through school. As a result of these disruptions, I finished school late, at age twenty. I started writing stories while I was still in school. I wrote a story based on an incident in my house and it was published in *Poonkothai*. After the story was published, some local members from the *Murpokku Ezhuthaalar Sangam* (Progressive Writers' Association) came and spoke to me. I began to fall in with people who were Left activists, thus beginning my engagement with Marxism.

NKR: Why did you think of becoming a writer when you were on the threshold of adulthood?

DB: When I left school in the late seventies, I had to start earning immediately to support my family. So I went to work in a dyeing factory in Erode. I worked there for a couple of years. The work was hard. After working twelve-hour shifts for six days, we were given one day off in a week, but the owner would ask me to come home and do his household work. I wrote a story based on this exploitative situation and it was published in *Taamarai*, a monthly magazine for workers published by CPI's literary wing. This gave me the confidence that I, too, could be a writer.

I also wrote a story about a school teacher pilfering grain supplied for the mid-day meal scheme. I was afraid that my father, a school teacher, would be upset. But as a seasoned reader, he appreciated the story for its craft and even recommended it to his colleagues at the school.

I made friends with people in the local trade unions and front organizations like DYFI, CITU and SYF. I also enrolled as a member of *Murpokku Ezhuthaalar Sangam* (Progressive Writers' Association) and *Makkal KalaiIlakkiya Kazhagam* (People's Art and Literary Organization).

During this time, I felt there was a chasm between art and reality. This was largely the result of the popular fiction I had read in my school days. With experience, I understood that art involved an imaginative transformation of reality.

NKR: 'Philosophers have always explained the world; the point is to change it,' Marx famously said. Did you believe that creative fiction was a means for changing the world? What kind of relationship did you envisage between a writer's imagination and the contingencies of the real world?

DB: Given my political engagement, I believed that literature could be an instrument for social transformation. I began to publish stories in literary journals of the left like *Vizhippu* (Vigilance), *Taamarai* (Lotus) and *Sigaram* (Peak). Well known leftist writers like D Selvaraj, Rajendra Chozhan and Poomani, Paa. Jeyapirakasam and Ponneelan were writing in those magazines. What we wrote was broadly on the lines of socialist realism, aimed at raising the revolutionary consciousness of workers and the common people.

I became more deeply involved with the activities of *Ma.Ka.E.Ka* (People's Association for Art and Literature) and contributed stories regularly to *Manavosai*, their literary journal. It was at this time that I was introduced to the set of writers who had pioneered modernist writing in Tamil. Since the fifties, there flourished an energetic'small magazine' movement in Tamilnadu, which was associated with the development of modernist writing. I read the leading writers of the genre: Sundara Ramaswamy, Thi Janakiraman and Ashokamitran. I also read all the back issues of *Kanaiyazhi, Ezhuthu, Ka Cha Tha Ta Pa Ra* and *Pragnai,* important literary journals of the sixties and seventies. The experience of reading such consciously literary works unsettled me and shook up the rather mechanistic notions I had about literature. Many of the modernist writers were Brahmins and I had met very few Brahmins in my life until then.

I also read the so-called *Karisal Ilakkiyam* (literature of the black soil), a branch of subaltern writing whose chief exponents were Ki Rajanarayanan, PaaJeyapirakasam and Poomani. All this reading considerably expanded my horizons and I learnt more about the possibilities inherent in writing fiction. I realized that fiction was more than a handy tool for achieving social transformation. Nor was fiction a mere recording of experience. Fiction could illuminate reality and engender an enhanced awareness. It could not transform reality directly, but it could affect the way readers experienced it.

NKR: Have your reasons for being a writer changed over the years? Could you talk about these changes?

DB: Around 1983, I also started attending literary conferences held in different parts of Tamilnadu. At the time, new directions were being forged in the milieu that went beyond modernism into structuralism and post-modernism. While I was absorbing these influences, I was introduced by a friend to the works of the great Russian masters – Turgenev, Dostoevsky, Tolstoy, Chekhov and Gorky – available in Tamil translation. In their works, I came across a profound examination of the human condition and societal arrangements. The fiction I then resolved to write had three defining qualities: it emerged from my storytelling instinct; it was engendered by a changing sense of the self; and it was an act of discovering the world, not the expression of a foregone conclusion.

I was particularly influenced by Tolstoy, who laid great emphasis on non-violence, moral sense and ethical conduct among men. In my own experience in the village, I had witnessed a lot of violence, cruelty and humiliation. The village is not the peaceful idyll that people think it is. The challenge of being a man under these conditions became the theme of my fiction. Given the influence Tolstoy had on Gandhi, I read writings on and by Gandhi as much as I could. Over the years, it had a profound influence on me. I began to look at what was happening around me, in the country and the world from a Gandhian perspective.

NKR: And what were the changes in the more practical dimensions of your life?

DB: My father passed away in 1983, while he was still in service.

As his eldest son, I was offered a clerical job on 'compassionate grounds' in the department of school education in 1985. This provided me with the much-needed economic stability. By then I had moved away from the Marxist-Leninist faction that I was involved with over differences on the use of violence as a strategy. I worked in the department for twenty years until I opted for voluntary retirement in 2006. I wrote and published stories through the next two decades. Meanwhile, I got married in 1986, and my marriage ended five years later.

In 2006, I joined *Kalachuvadu*, a leading literary journal in Tamil, as executive editor, and worked there for six years. In 2013, I worked as script-writer for television programmes in a media organization. This was my last job before I turned to full-time writing earlier this year.

NKR: Your first novel, *Nizhalin Thanimai* (The Loneliness of a Shadow), arrived more than thirty years after you started writing. Why did you choose the short story as your preferred form over a long period? What new possibilities does the novel form offer you?

DB: When I started writing fiction, I found that the short story form was very convenient for recording the life of people around me. The short story is very good for reflecting, as through the shards of a broken mirror, what a writer observes of the world, for creating moments of epiphany around commonplace events. Using the short story form, it is possible to explore a diverse range of characters and situations. It is also possible to experiment with many modes and styles of narration, apart from different registers of a language. Given my early political orientation, it was natural that I fell in with the short story form.

As I grew older, I felt the need for writing narratives with expanded scope, for the ability to deal with the flow of life and destinies of various characters over a longer period. I also found that I wanted to reflect the essential plurality of the world within a single narrative. All this is possible only through the novel. It is for this reason that I have focused my current efforts on novel writing. It is the form of choice at this stage in my life.

NKR: Stories written around certain incidents in Gandhi's life are not uncommon in contemporary Indian literature. Stories around heroic figures are but a natural extension of our oral tradition in storytelling. The eponymous story in this collection, 'Farewell, Mahatma' was received very well when it was originally published in Tamil. What made you attempt a story based on Gandhi's life? What aspect of the twenty-first century does the story relate to?

DB: My engagement with the works of Tolstoy and Gandhi in the late-eighties led me to believe that the struggle for morality and compassion was the most essential feature of the life of mankind. My work has been animated by this belief ever since.

'Farewell, Mahatma' came out of a particular historical moment. I am referring to the so-called post-Godhra riots in Gujarat in February-March 2002, where a few thousand innocent, defenceless Muslims were murdered by violent mobs. I was deeply distressed and troubled that an event of such unimaginable cruelty and moral failure could take place in our own time. Later that year, during the arts festival in the school where I was employed, many among the students dressed up as Gandhi for the annual fancy dress competition. I recognized that Gandhi was very much alive in the imagination of our children, but his spirit seemed to have vanished from our public space. It also occurred to me that there could be many versions of Gandhi in a society caught up in a tangle of moral confusion. I wondered whether the Gujarat riots would have taken place had Mahatma

Gandhi been alive in our midst. I wanted to discover, through my imagination, how the spirit of Gandhi came to be extinguished from our land. 'Farewell, Mahatma' is my fictional account of who we have become as a country in relation to the life and spirit of Mahatma Gandhi.

NKR: A recurring theme in your stories is the precarious nature of man-woman relationships, the attendant tension, suspicion and hatred between the sexes. Is this your response to a contemporary situation?

DB: It is very much a concern that belongs with the present. As we have entered the era of modernity, the old morality of pre-modern times, especially the one governing relations between the sexes, has slowly faded away. A new morality is yet to form itself and take its place. This is because although we are outwardly modern, we have yet to become modern in the depths of our existence. My stories are a way of sounding the alarm about the troubles brewing in and around us, as well as a hint of what the future may hold.

NKR: The lives and traits of working class people in the rural areas have a special place in your work. You write just as evocatively about urban people. Can you say more about this diversity?

DB: In my life, I have alternated several times between village and city. So I have a reasonable grasp of both environments. Perhaps I am closer to the rural way of life than the average city-dweller. I believe that the human struggle in both settings is ultimately the same, only the material and social contexts differ to some extent. In both places, people are subjugated by a power structure that they cannot easily question or challenge. I write with equal concern for both, and without a marked preference for either.

NKR: Social structure in India is largely based on caste hierarchy and divisions. What is the place of caste relations in literary fiction? Should we speak about it openly? What potential changes can such work bring about in society?

DB: Caste is very definitely a huge factor in our social relations. It cannot be ignored or glossed over. However, caste boundaries and the relationship between castes haven't remained the same over the years. The advent of modern institutions in our society has given rise to new conflicts and contradictions in which caste plays a complex role, with renewed vigour. A writer must be aware of this new morphology of caste, especially in our urban areas. Acknowledging this new-fangled social presence of caste through our writing will be of great epistemic value, especially to the young and future generations.

NKR: In modern Tamil literature, the so-called upper caste writers were the pioneers. Later, people of the oppressed castes not only started to write but also inhabited fictional spaces as characters. Since the lifestyle and culture of these people were not so widely known, this category of fiction features ethnographic elements in order to make the characters intelligible and even for the sake of verisimilitude. But in your fiction, such ethnographic details are very minimal. Could you say why?

DB: Ever since caste has assumed a position of renewed importance in contemporary electoral politics and in the competition for public resources, there has been a strand in modern Tamil writing that seeks to retrieve the glories of a lost tradition or even to invent or embellish them as necessary, all in the interests of particular caste groups. We often find that through these ethnographic descriptions, a writer betrays a clear alignment with his own caste group, losing sight of the wider human reality or concerns. It's true that anything can be described in literary fiction, including caste rituals, customs and festivals, but such writing should not serve to reinforce caste divisions and promote regressive politics. It is for this reason that I try to portray the reality of human relations, including relations between castes, as they exist, without giving undue importance to ethnographic details.

NKR: You have been the executive editor of an important literary magazine for more than five years. You've been writing essays on politics and current affairs regularly. How can such journalistic skills and work help a creative writer?

DB: Being a magazine editor has contributed, albeit indirectly, in several ways. I have had to keep myself up to date on the socio-political environment and on public issues of the day in a disciplined and systematic manner. Writing for a magazine involves developing the required language skills and editing the material for conciseness and clarity, which are very important qualities for any practising writer. Moreover, one is constantly reading and discussing the latest works to appear in the milieu, which is enormously rewarding and enriching for a writer.

NKR: Your memoir, *A Few Sketches in the Dust,* **documents the shifting political moods and activism of people in a backward rural area with wit and humour. Such efforts are actually quite rare in Tamil. Why don't you write more such long-form, first-person journalistic accounts?**

DB: As I've said earlier, I was involved in a political movement through which I met a lot of people, both activists and common village folk. I discovered that people in the rural areas possessed a high degree of political awareness, which was limited only by the possibilities of their social and material contexts. The two memoir-like narratives in *A Few Sketches...* are attempts to present this environment as refracted through my own personal experiences.

I certainly want to write about certain milieus I have experienced in the course of my life. For example, I would like to write first-person accounts of the Marxist-Leninist movement in Tamilnadu in the eighties, the school education system and the vagaries of the Tamil film industry.

NKR: You have tried your hand at writing plays and film scripts. Could you tell us something about these efforts?

DB: Many relatives on my mother's side were famous koothu artistes in the Kongu region. So I grew up watching a lot of performance theatre as a child. Later, when I was with the People's Association for Art and Literature, we did a lot of street theatre performances as part of our programme of work. Therefore, I was quite familiar with the conventions and mechanics of modern theatre. This led to my participation later in a couple of play-writing workshops conducted by the National School of Drama in Pondicherry. I wrote a play, which was selected by the Sangeet-Natak Akademi for its young playwright award. However, plays need to be staged. Because of the paucity of groups to stage modern Tamil plays in our state, I knew that any plays that I might write would have only a slim chance of reaching an audience. Therefore, I was not inclined to write more plays. However, the playwright's technique of moving characters around in closed spaces and creating moods is something I use in my stories. Even this collection has a few stories in which I have used the technique.

I wrote the story for a Tamil film which was produced over two years in the late-nineties. I involved myself in all aspects of film-making. The experience made it obvious to me that I could never work with the medium. So I returned to writing fiction.

NKR: How did you arrive at the language and style of your fiction?

DB: In the initial stages, a writer tends to imitate the language and styles of the writers he admires. But it is indeed a challenge to find your own voice to suit the material that you are moved to write about. For this, you need a special language that is unique to your own spirit. I believe that each person has a right to language, and it is up to the writer to discover and claim that right in the process of writing.

NKR: What works have you planned for the future?

DB: I am currently at work on two novels. The first, *Noyyal*, is a multi-generational tale of a family that lived in the area between the banks of Noyyal and Amaravathi rivers in Kongunadu, my native region. *Virodhi*, the second novel, is a political novel. I expect to complete both novels in the next twelve months.

(The conversation, which happened originally in Tamil, was translated into English by N Kalyan Raman)

Translator's Note

In India, we've had a long tradition of *telling* stories. No surprise, then, that narrative style in modernist fiction, when it came to be written over a century ago, was strongly inflected by speech rhythms. In Tamil, a famously diglossic language, both diction and speech rhythms varied with region, class and, most importantly, with caste. This led to an informal 'enclave' mentality among the early practitioners, most of them hailing from the upper castes. The space of modernist literature, as with the province of classical texts, remained inaccessible to large sections of Tamil society.

It was only after the passage of fifty years, during which Tamil society was subject to transformative changes, that narrative fiction in Tamil began to employ a contemporary prose style that was accessible by all Tamil-speaking people. Naturally, this came about gradually, with more and more writers from all quarters switching to a common prose style over time. The same period also saw the emergence of sub-regional literature, or *vattarailakkiyam,* which combined formal narration with the distinctive cultural inflections and speech rhythms of different communities.

As someone who began writing in the early eighties, Devibharathi came directly to the secular prose style of the modernists. His approach to narrative language eschews special emphasis on the anthropological-ethnographic dimension, because he feels that it accentuates the existing differences between communities and reifies them in a way. His diction, even in dialogues, is simple, formal and direct. His attempt is to tell a human story every time, remaining true to its context while taking care not to embellish it to a degree where it overshadows the irreducible humanity of his characters.

The stories in this collection vary widely in their contexts. Village and small-town life is depicted in 'The Tool of His Trade', 'Staying Alive' and 'Remains'. In 'The Curse of Resurrection', a folktale from the distant past is given a new lease of life even as the charm and mystery of its folk origins is preserved intact. Of the others, 'Reversal' and 'Ruin' explore the dark recesses of the contemporary individual, besieged by unsettling modernity, particularly in that brittle, volatile space between man and woman. 'Farewell, Mahatma' is a wholly imagined reconstruction of recent history, belonging nowhere in particular and everywhere. In 'Victim', the author employs a traditional narrator who narrates and explicates the story at the same time, impersonating the kattiyakkaran (or sutradhar in North India) of traditional Tamil theatre in Tamilnadu.

Given the diversity of contexts and simplicity of language, the most distinctive aspect of these stories is Devibharathi's superb craft as a storyteller, something the reader will experience on every page. I enjoyed translating Devibharathi's self-consciously modern 'voice', made up of context, language and craft. I hope the reader will experience as much pleasure in reading them.

N. Kalyan Raman
December 2014

Devibharathi was born and raised in a small village in western Tamil Nadu. He worked as a political activist, government employee, journalist, managing editor of a leading literary magazine and scriptwriter for television programmes. During his writing career, spanning more than forty years, Devibharathi published two collections of short stories, two novellas, four novels, a play and two non-fiction anthologies containing essays and memoirs. He has received several awards, including the inaugural Tannaram Literary Award in 2021 and the Kalaignar Porkizhi Award 2023 for literary excellence. He lives and works in a village in Tamil Nadu's Tirupur district.

N. Kalyan Raman is a translator of contemporary Tamil fiction and poetry into English. Over the past twenty-five years, he has published translations of fourteen works of Tamil fiction by important writers such as Ashokamitran, Poomani, Devibharathi, Perumal Murugan, Vaasanthi and Salma. His translation of Perumal Murugan's *Poonachi* was shortlisted for the inaugural JCB Prize (2018), longlisted for the National Book Award for Translated Literature (2020) in the US, and was awarded the Sahitya Akademi Translation Prize in English (2022). In 2017, he received the prestigious Pudumaipithan Award for his contribution to the cause of Tamil literature.

HARPERPERENNIAL

Harper Perennial presents special editions of its finest books in translation

Apradhini
Shivani
Translated from the Hindi by Ira Pande

Avasthe
U.R. Ananthamurthy
Translated from the Kannada by Narayan Hegde

Blue Is Like Blue
Vinod Kumar Shukla
Translated from the Hindi by Arvind Krishna Mehrotra and Sara Rai

Diary of a Malayali Madman
N. Prabhakaran
Translated from the Malayalam by Jayasree Kalathil

Farewell, Mahatma
Devibharathi
Translated from the Tamil by N. Kalyan Raman

The Golden Gandhi Statue from America
Subimal Misra
Translated from the Bengali by V. Ramaswamy

A Name for Every Leaf
Ashok Vajpeyi
Translated from the Hindi by Rahul Soni

Moustache
S. Hareesh
Translated from the Malayalam by Jayasree Kalathil

Seven Sixes Are Forty-Three
Kiran Nagarkar
Translated from the Marathi by Shubha Slee

Shameless
Taslima Nasreen
Translated from the Bengali by Arunava Sinha

HARPERPERENNIAL

Age of Frenzy
Mahabaleshwar Sail
Translated from the Konkani by Vidya Pai

A Life Incomplete
Nanak Singh
Translated from the Punjabi by Navdeep Suri

Mohanaswamy
Vasudhendra
Translated from the Kannada by Rashmi Terdal

The Music of Solitude
Krishna Sobti
Translated from the Hindi by Vasudha Dalmia

No Presents Please
Jayant Kaikini
Translated from the Kannada by Tejaswini Niranjana

A Preface to Man
Subhash Chandran
Translated from the Malayalam by Fathima E.V.

The Secret Garland
Andal
Translated from the Tamil by Archana Venkatesan

Shala
Milind Bokil
Translated from the Marathi by Vikrant Pande

The Weary Generations
Abdullah Hussein
Translated from the Urdu by the author

Written in Tears
Arupa Patangia Kalita
Translated from the Assamese by Ranjita Biswas

HARPERPERENNIAL

Bhima
M.T. Vasudevan Nair
Translated from the Malayalam by Gita Krishnankutty

Chemmeen
Thakazhi Sivasankara Pillai
Translated from the Malayalam by Anita Nair

Ghachar Ghochar
Vivek Shanbhag
Translated from the Kannada by Srinath Perur

Hindutva or Hind Swaraj
U.R. Ananthamurthy
Translated from the Kannada by Keerti Ramachandra and Vivek Shanbhag

The Liberation of Sita
Volga
Translated from the Telugu by T. Vijay Kumar and C. Vijayasree

A Life Misspent
Suryakant Tripathi Nirala
Translated from the Hindi by Satti Khanna

The Sea Lies Ahead
Intizar Husain
Translated from the Urdu by Rakhshanda Jalil

Selected Poems
Joy Goswami
Translated from the Bengali by Sampurna Chattarji

Wild Animals Prohibited
Subimal Misra
Translated from the Bengali by V. Ramaswamy

Wild Words
Malathi Maithri, Salma, Kutti Revathi and Sukirtharani
Translated from the Tamil by Lakshmi Holmström

HarperCollins *Publishers* India

At HarperCollins India, we believe in telling the best stories and finding the widest readership for our books in every format possible. We started publishing in 1992; a great deal has changed since then, but what has remained constant is the passion with which our authors write their books, the love with which readers receive them, and the sheer joy and excitement that we as publishers feel in being a part of the publishing process.

Over the years, we've had the pleasure of publishing some of the finest writing from the subcontinent and around the world, including several award-winning titles and some of the biggest bestsellers in India's publishing history. But nothing has meant more to us than the fact that millions of people have read the books we published, and that somewhere, a book of ours might have made a difference.

As we look to the future, we go back to that one word—a word which has been a driving force for us all these years.

Read.